Are You
Terrified Yet?

Look for more books in the Goosebumps Series 2000
by R.L. Stine:

Are You Terrified Yet?

AN
APPLE
PAPERBACK

SCHOLASTIC INC.
New York Toronto London Auckland Sydney

A PARACHUTE PRESS BOOK

ISBN 0-590-39996-9

Copyright © 1998 by Parachute Press, Inc.
All rights reserved. Published by Scholastic Inc.
APPLE PAPERBACKS and logo are trademarks and/or registered trademarks of Scholastic Inc.
GOOSEBUMPS is a registered trademark
of Parachute Press, Inc.

12 11 10 9 8 7 6 5 4 3 2 1   8 9/9 0 1 2 3/0

Printed in the U.S.A.   40

First Scholastic printing, September 1998

Are You Terrified Yet?

I let out a scream as the huge insect scraped the back of my neck. I could feel its pincers prickle my skin.

My hand shot up to my neck. I grabbed the bug. "Whoooa!" I nearly toppled off my bike.

I braked hard. Caught my balance.

And stared down at the brown leaf crinkled in my hand.

A leaf? A dead leaf?

Not a huge, disgusting insect.

"Oh, wow." With a groan, I crumpled the leaf and tossed it to the street.

Craig, remember your promise, I scolded myself. You're starting a new school — and a new life. You never heard the word *wimp* before. You never heard the name *Fraidy Cat.*

That's all in the past, I reminded myself. You left those names behind at your old school.

Starting today, you're going to be *brave*, Craig. You're going to be fearless.

You're going to be a *superhero*!

My bike tire crunched over the brown leaf as I shifted gears and started pedaling again. I shook my head.

Craig, how will you ever be a superhero if you scream because a leaf scrapes your neck?

Well . . . it was a *pretty big* leaf, I told myself.

Do you ever have conversations with yourself on the way to school in the morning? Do you ever talk to yourself about what you plan to do and not do?

Well, I do. My name is Craig Morgenstern. I turned twelve a few weeks ago.

My family moved to Middle Valley, a little town in Ohio that you've probably never heard of. It's not in the *middle* of anything, and it doesn't even have a *valley*. But Middle Valley means a *lot* to me.

It means I can start a whole new life.

Know what the kids at my old school called me? C-C-C-Craig.

That's because I stammer when I'm frightened. And since I'm frightened all the time, I stammer a lot.

C-C-C-Craig.

They thought that was so funny. But every time

someone called me that, I just wanted to sink into the ground and disappear forever.

Some people are braver than others — and just about everyone is braver than me.

Maybe it's because most kids my age are bigger than me. I'm short and very skinny. I have crazy brown hair that refuses to stay down. Most of the time, my *hair* looks as if it's standing straight up in fright!

Kids at my old school loved to make me scream.

They would jump out at me from their lockers. And sneak up behind me and pinch me. Or drop bugs and worms and things down my back.

I won't even tell you what they did to me last Halloween. I start to shake just thinking about it.

But that's old news.

No way anyone at Middle Valley Middle School will ever call me C-C-C-Craig.

Because I'm the new me.

Of course I felt nervous starting a new school. My hands were cold and sweaty on the handlebars of my bike. My leg muscles kept cramping up as I pedaled downhill.

But *nervous* is normal — right? *Nervous* isn't the same as *scared*.

The morning breeze felt cool on my hot cheeks. The sun was still a red ball, floating low over the rooftops. The leaves shimmering on the trees were bright shades of red and yellow. Fall had started early this year.

A maroon van filled with kids and dogs rumbled past me. The dogs barked and frantically pawed the back window as the van rolled by.

I shifted gears again. The hill leading down to the school was pretty steep.

I crossed a street and passed a group of kids. It was easy to tell this was the first day of school. They were all talking at once, very excited. And their backpacks were all new and clean and stiff-looking.

Most of the kids seemed to be about my age. I wondered if any of them would be my friends.

I watched them cross the street, thinking about how hard it is to make new friends.

I should have kept my eye on the road.

My front tire hit something — a rock, I think. Before I could cry out or catch my balance, the bike skidded . . . skidded . . . and toppled over.

My hands flew up.

I hit the pavement hard.

Pain shot up my side.

The bike fell on top of me. One handlebar jabbed into my ribs.

I groaned and waited for the pain to fade. Then I started to push the bike off me.

But before I could move, I saw a blue car rolling down the hill.

I heard a baby cry. A high, shrill wail . . . from the backseat.

4

And behind the wheel — *nobody!*
No driver. No driver . . .
The baby screaming.
The car rolling faster now, about to run right over me.

I froze in panic.

But the baby's scream forced me to move. My arms and legs all kicked out at once, like a bug on its back.

I shoved the bike off me and jumped to my feet.

The blue car rolled faster. It looked like a roller-coaster car zooming down a track.

Hunched in the middle of the street, I blinked once. Twice. Trying to make a driver appear behind the wheel.

But no. No driver.

And the car rolled toward me. A few feet away. The baby howling in terror.

I heard another cry — and raised my eyes to the top of the hill. "My baby! My baby!" A red-haired woman came running frantically down the hill, both arms churning the air, her yellow jacket flying behind her like a cape.

I sucked in a deep breath. And moved to the driver's side.

Here it comes! Here it comes!

I didn't think. No time to make a plan.

I readied myself. Tightened every muscle. Timed it . . . timed it . . .

As the car rolled past, I grabbed for the door handle.

And missed.

"Oh, no!" A cry escaped my throat as my hand hit the door.

I made a wild leap.

Hit the side of the car and bounced off. I landed on my knees at the side of the street.

"Noooooo!"

I heard others screaming now. And glimpsed the red-haired woman, her hands pumping, her scream like a chant: "My baby! *My baby!*"

I turned to see the car rolling faster now, rocketing down the hill — to an intersection. I saw a red traffic light. Kids crossing. The intersection crowded with kids.

Craig, get moving! I ordered myself. Save that baby!

I forced my legs to run. Stumbling, staggering, I chased after the car. Off-balance, my head spinning, the baby's shrill wails ringing in my ears, I caught up with the car.

Ran alongside it.

Reached out both hands. Stretched . . .

Stretched for the door handle.

No. I can't reach it, I saw. I can't catch it.

I can't . . .

Down below, I saw kids crossing the street.

"Look out! Look out!" I screamed to them.

Inside the car, I saw tiny pink hands waving wildly in the backseat.

I struggled to run faster.

I reached out . . . reached out . . .

Missed again.

hen I grabbed it. My hand tightened around the handle.

Running as fast as I could to keep up with the car, I pulled open the car door.

I leaped headfirst into the front seat.

The baby wailed and thrashed its little arms. It squirmed and struggled in its car seat.

I pushed myself up. Gasping, I lowered my foot. It bumped the brake pedal.

I raised my foot — and slammed it down hard.

The car lurched. And rocked to a stop.

I bounced forward. My head hit the windshield.

"Ohhh." Pain shot down my body. I shut my eyes.

The hard jolt of the car made the baby stop crying. Outside, I could hear kids shouting. Loud cries of surprise and alarm.

I did it, I realized. I stopped the car in time.

I could feel the blood pulsing at my temples. I felt so dizzy . . . so dizzy, I couldn't hold my head up.

Everything went bright red. The red faded to white. A throbbing white light.

I think I started to faint.

But the mother's shouts snapped me awake. "My baby! My baby!"

The back door flew open. The red-haired woman leaned into the car. She unfastened the baby and lifted it in her arms.

I sat behind the wheel, still gasping for breath. My whole body started to quake and shake.

Did I really do that? I asked myself.

I climbed dizzily out of the car. I rubbed my forehead. It still ached from bumping the windshield.

Kids surrounded the car, all talking at once, all staring at me.

Hugging her baby tight, the woman came hurrying over to me.

"That's the bravest thing I ever saw!" she declared. She hugged me with her free hand. "You are a hero!"

I could feel my face growing hot, and I knew I was blushing.

Me? A *hero*?

Some kids started to cheer. Someone slapped me on the back.

The woman had tears running down her face. "I got out of the car to mail a letter," she explained. "I didn't see the car rolling downhill. It . . . it could have been a tragedy."

"Yeah. I guess . . . ," I murmured. I didn't know what to say.

I think I was in shock. My head was spinning. I couldn't feel my feet touching the ground. I was *numb*!

The woman shifted the baby to her other arm. Then she turned to the crowd. "Did you see what this boy did? He jumped off his bike and threw his body against the car to stop it!"

Well . . . that wasn't exactly right. Not exactly the way it happened. But with everyone staring and clapping and talking, I didn't feel like arguing.

"He was nearly killed!" the woman exclaimed, wiping away tears. "But he risked his life to save my baby and all the kids in the street. I never saw anything so brave!"

Another loud cheer rose up.

I jammed my hands into my jeans pockets, trying to stop from shaking.

I didn't feel brave. I didn't feel like a hero. I knew that my big rescue was pretty much an accident.

I mean, I didn't *jump* off my bike. I *fell*!

And then, when I saw that car coming at me, I didn't know *what* I was doing!

As the crowd cheered and congratulated me, I

felt like confessing. *It was all just an accident. I'm not really brave!*

But I kept my mouth shut. I forced a modest smile.

This is your big chance, Craig, I told myself. This is a lucky moment for you. This is your chance to make sure that no one ever calls you C-C-C-Craig again.

The woman hugged me again. She leaned into the car and started to strap in the baby.

Someone tapped me on the shoulder. I spun around.

I stared at a girl with black curly hair and round black eyes.

"Are you the new kid in the sixth grade?" she asked. She had a smooth, low voice, a grownup's voice. "I heard there was a new kid in our class this year."

She wore a black vest over a white top, a short black skirt over black tights.

I nodded. "I guess." If only I could get my heart to stop racing. And my legs to stop trembling.

"I'm in your class," she announced. "I'm Amy Suskind."

She introduced me to the two guys with her — Travis Walker and Brad Caperton. "They're in our class too," Amy said.

"I'm Craig Morgenstern," I told them, my voice still breathless and shaky.

12

Travis and Brad gazed at me suspiciously. They were both tall and lean.

Brad had short, spiky dark hair. He wore a black denim jacket, a blue T-shirt, and faded jeans, torn at both knees.

Travis had freckles on his nose and cheeks. He had intense green eyes. He wore a Cleveland Indians cap pulled down low over his forehead. A tiny silver ring gleamed in one earlobe.

Amy's round dark eyes peered into mine. "Craig, are you *always* this brave?" she asked.

"Uh . . . yeah. I guess so," I replied.

Brad narrowed his eyes at me. His lips formed a sneer. "You mean you do stuff like this all the time?"

I cleared my throat. "Well, yeah," I said. "I try to. It keeps me from getting bored."

What am I saying? I asked myself.

Why am I acting like such a jerk?

I guess I wanted to take advantage of this lucky accident. No more C-C-C-Craig. Not ever again.

Little did I know how much *total terror* my bragging would bring me.

Little did I know that my words would lead me into a *coffin*.

locker door slammed behind me. I jumped a mile.

I instantly spun around to check if anyone had seen me jump.

It was the second day of school, and I was enjoying my new role as hero.

Kids I didn't know waved and nodded to me in the hall. In the lunchroom on Monday, I heard a tableful of really cute girls talking about me. They kept glancing over to my table and smiling.

Even some of the teachers flashed me a thumbs-up as I passed them in the halls.

Craig, this is *excellent*, I told myself.

I think I'm going to like it here!

I caught myself strutting to class. I had to remind myself not to get *too* carried away.

Deep down inside, you're still C-C-C-Craig, I told myself.

Amy and Travis came around the corner, bumping each other playfully, trying to slam one another into the wall.

"Everyone is still talking about what you did yesterday," Amy said, giving Travis a hard bump that sent him flying.

"Oh, that was nothing," I bragged. "Really. What's the big deal?"

She laughed, tossing back her black curls. Her dark eyes flashed. I could see how much she admired me. I could see she looked up to me — even though she was six inches taller!

She thinks you're great, Craig, I told myself. Don't blow it.

Travis straightened his backpack on his shoulders. "You want to do something brave?" he asked.

"Well . . ." I hesitated.

Travis motioned across the hall. "Help Brad beat up his big brother."

Amy and I followed Travis's gaze. Across the hall, a big, athletic-looking guy was shoving Brad into an open locker. Brad was struggling and squirming. But the big guy was too strong for him.

"That's Brad's brother?" I murmured. He looks really tough, I thought.

Sometimes I'm glad I'm an only child.

"That's Grant," Amy said in a whisper.

"He thinks because he's in ninth grade he can push Brad around," Travis explained, frowning.

I shuddered as Grant shoved Brad all the way into the locker and slammed the door. A big grin on his face, Grant turned and stomped away. The floor seemed to shake under his heavy footsteps.

I turned and found Amy and Travis both staring at me.

"Uh ... Brad just has to stand up to his brother," I said.

How lame can you get?

"Brad shouldn't let himself be pushed around," I added. "I know I never would!"

Why did I say that?

Why am I acting like such a big shot?

The three of us hurried across the hall. Travis pulled open the locker, and we tugged Brad out.

He appeared dazed. He shook himself like a dog trying to get dry and blinked several times.

"Craig says you have to stand up to your brother," Amy reported.

"Excuse me?" Brad turned to me. "You want to help me stand up to him?"

"Well ..." I swallowed my bubblegum.

Careful, Craig, I warned myself. They already think you're brave. You don't have to prove it again.

How wrong can a person be?

*   *   *

16

I was walking home after school, humming to myself, feeling good. The red and yellow leaves shimmered in a warm breeze, warm as spring. The sun beamed down in a clear blue sky.

I started up the steep hill. I had just passed the corner where my daring rescue had taken place when I heard an urgent call. "Craig — hey! Stop! Craig!"

I turned and saw Amy running along the sidewalk, her backpack bouncing wildly on her shoulders. "Craig — help!"

Help?

"What's up?" I asked, trying to sound casual.

"Quick — over here." She grabbed my arm and tugged me around the corner. "Hurry!"

"What's up?" I repeated. I had a sinking feeling in my stomach. Why did Amy look so upset? What was so urgent?

Across the street, I spotted a girl of about six or seven standing under a tall tree. I saw a lunch box and a red jacket on the ground beside her. She stared up into the tree, pointing furiously and shaking her head.

"Hurry," Amy repeated, tugging me across the street.

As we came nearer, I could hear the girl crying.

"Wh-what's the problem?" I asked breathlessly.

Sobbing hard, the girl pointed up to a high branch. "My brother —" she choked out between sobs.

"He's up there," Amy told me.

"Excuse me?" I started to back away. But Amy blocked my path.

"Her little brother climbed the tree, and now he can't get down," Amy explained.

"Too bad," I murmured. I gazed up into the leafy branches. I could see legs and two sneakers dangling from a high limb.

"What are we going to do?" the girl wailed.

"Get me down!" a high voice called from up in the tree.

Amy placed a comforting hand on the girl's trembling shoulder. "Don't worry," she said. "We have a superhero right here."

Huh? Me? I thought.

That sinking feeling in my stomach became a tight, hard knot. I suddenly felt really sick.

"No problem," Amy told the girl. "Craig will climb up and bring your brother down in seconds. Craig is so brave. He does this kind of thing all the time."

"Oh, wow," I murmured. I gazed up at the dangling sneakers. How did the kid climb so high?

My stomach churned. I'm *totally* afraid of heights.

I mean, I get nauseous on escalators!

Amy gave me a shove toward the tree. "Go ahead, Craig. Hurry! Bring the poor kid down," she urged.

I could feel cold sweat rolling down my forehead. I wiped my clammy hands on the legs of my khakis.

"Stop crying," Amy told the girl softly. "Craig will take care of everything. Right, Craig? Tell her."

"Right," I choked out. My voice cracked on the word.

I stared up at the dangling sneakers.

"Get me down! Get me down!" the little boy wailed.

Amy and the girl were both watching me.

I wiped off my cold, sweaty hands again. And stared up at the high tree limb.

I can't do this, I realized.

I've never climbed a tree in my life.

No way I can get up there. And if I do get up there, no way I can bring the kid down.

I'll fall and break every bone in my skinny, cowardly body.

What can I do?

What?

 glanced back and saw kids running from all directions. A crowd gathered around the tree.

"Is the boy okay?"

"How did he get up there?"

"Is he stuck up there?"

Alarmed voices all around.

"It's okay. No problem," Amy assured everyone loudly. "Craig is going to bring him down."

I swallowed hard. Everyone turned to stare at me.

Craig, you have no choice now, I told myself. You have to go up and rescue that kid.

If you don't, you'll be C-C-C-Craig at Middle Valley Middle School for the rest of your days.

I swallowed again. My legs were shaking so

hard, I thought my pants would fall down! I hoped Amy couldn't see the terrified expression on my face.

I wrapped my arms around the tree trunk.

Ow. The jagged bark scraped my hands.

I can't do this, I realized.

"Help me! I'm sooooo scared!" The little boy called down. "Please — help me! The branch — it's breaking! It's *breaking*!"

Behind me, kids gasped and screamed.

Over the sound of their screams, I heard a loud *CRAAAAAACK*.

My whole body shuddered.

"Hurry!" Amy cried.

"The tree is *breaking*!" the little boy wailed.

Another *CRAAAACK* made everyone gasp and cry out again.

I wiped my sweaty hands. "Hold on tight up there!" I boomed, trying to sound brave. "I'm coming up!"

"Hurry! Hurry!" Kids were shrieking.

Another *CRAAAACK*, like Velcro tearing.

I grabbed the trunk again. And lifted my feet off the ground. Slowly, carefully, I hoisted myself onto the lowest limb, only a few feet off the ground.

Whew. So far, so good.

Why didn't the kid stop here? I wondered.

I swung myself up. My hands were so wet, they nearly slid off the branch.

I grabbed for the next limb — and got a mouth-ful of leaves.

Yuck.

"Help me!" The boy's cries were still high above me. "Help! I can't hold on any longer! It's break-ing! It's *breaking*!"

"I'm . . . coming!" I choked out.

I hoisted myself onto the next limb. Then I forced my legs to stop shaking and stood up.

Hugging the trunk tight, I worked my way around to the back of the tree. I found a limb a few feet above my head. Grabbed it. Pulled my-self up.

Yes!

"Hurry! Ohh . . . hurry!" The frightened boy sounded a little closer.

"I'm . . . almost . . . there," I called up to him.

"I can't hold on! I can't!"

Taking a deep breath, I pulled myself higher. I could see his sneakers clearly now, dangling, his legs kicking. Just a few branches above me.

"I'm . . . coming! Hold on!" I gasped.

I hoisted myself higher. Higher.

Until I reached the limb where he sat.

He turned to me, his round, little face red as a tomato, glistening with tears. His blond hair standing up in wild tufts. His T-shirt dirty and ripped at one shoulder.

"Hold on," I uttered. "I'm here. Just hold on."

Slowly . . . slowly . . . I worked my way out on the limb. Farther. Almost there . . . Almost . . .

I reached out both hands to grab him.

"I've got you —!" I whispered.

My hands were inches from him — when he fell.

I watched his hands fly up as he slipped off the branch.

"Nooooooo!" a scream of horror burst from my throat.

I cut it short when I realized the kid didn't fall.

He grabbed another limb. Grabbed it and dove to the trunk.

Then as I gaped in shock, he slid easily down the trunk to the ground.

He landed softly on his feet.

Peering down through the leaves, I saw his sister wrap him in a hug.

Loud cries and cheers rang out.

Then, over the ringing cheers, I heard a terrifying sound.

Another *CRAAAAACK*.

So close now.

Another *CRAAAACK*. Right under me!

It took less than a second.

I heard the *CRAAAACK*. Then I felt a rush of air as I started to fall.

"Hey —!" I let out a cry. And shot up both hands. Grabbed for the limb above me.

My hands wrapped around it.

No. I missed the limb.

My hands wrapped around — a bird's nest!

I glimpsed the nest.

I heard myself scream. A high, long scream.

And then I hit the ground. Hard.

I think I landed on my stomach. I'm really not sure.

I remember the *THUD*. The pain. And then, blackness.

I guess I had my wind knocked out.

When I opened my eyes, I found myself on my side, staring down at the grass. The ground appeared to tilt, first one way, then the other.

I held on. Held on.

What was I holding? I struggled to focus. I was still holding onto the empty bird's nest.

I blinked several times. The ground finally stopped tilting.

I uttered a long sigh. Craig, you didn't save the kid, I told myself. He saved himself.

And now Amy knows what a total klutz you are. Amy and everyone else.

Still on the ground, I glanced up. I saw the girl

walking off with her brother. He was laughing. She held his hand tightly.

I heard voices. Excited voices, all talking at once.

And over them, I heard Amy. "Craig is unbelievable!"

Did I hear right? What was she saying?

I pulled myself up with a groan and tried to listen.

"Isn't Craig awesome?" Amy exclaimed. "First he showed that little boy how to slide down. Then, when the tree branch broke off, he rescued the bird's nest!"

"Huh?" I muttered, still groggy. "*What* did I do?"

"Craig didn't even think of his own safety," Amy declared. "He only thought of rescuing the nest!"

That's not quite the way it happened, I thought.

But before I could protest, kids were pulling me to my feet, slapping me on the back, congratulating me, clapping and cheering.

"Bravest thing I ever saw," a woman told a gray-uniformed mail carrier.

He nodded. "Someone should tell the mayor. That boy ought to get an award."

"He risked his life to save a bird's nest. Wow," the woman said.

More cheers. More slaps on the back. More high fives.

Amy gazed down at me with that glowing, ad-

26

miring look in her eyes. "Awesome," she murmured. "Awesome."

And then a boy's voice rang out. "Hey, wait!"

I turned and saw Travis and Brad pushing through the surprised crowd.

"What is your *problem*? Craig isn't brave!" Travis declared.

Brad sneered. "He's a total phony!"

Amy and the other kids gasped.

I'm caught, I realized. They found me out.

I'm C-C-C-Craig again.

My life is ruined.

I took a step back. I suddenly wanted to be back up in the tree, far, far away.

"What are you *saying*?" Amy demanded angrily, pressing her hands to her waist.

"He wasn't being brave," Travis repeated. "I think he *fell* out of that tree."

"For sure," Brad agreed. "I saw the whole thing."

"But — but —" Amy sputtered.

"If he was being brave, why did he scream like that?" Brad demanded.

"Yeah," Travis agreed. "He screamed all the way down. He fell out of a tree — and you act as if he's some kind of hero!"

All three of them turned to me. As if they expected me to settle the argument for them.

Craig, are you brave or not?

Not.

I just shrugged. "Whatever," I murmured. "What I did up there, it was no big deal."

"Right — it was no big deal!" Travis accused. "You fell out of a tree. That's all you did!"

"You're just jealous." Amy sneered at Travis and Brad. "Both of you. You two got all the attention before Craig arrived."

Travis and Brad pushed her out of the way and stepped up to me. They narrowed their eyes menacingly.

A staring contest.

I never win staring contests. I always blink.

"You really think you're so brave?" Travis challenged.

"Me?" I choked out. "No. No way."

I wasn't going to get into a fight over this. For one thing, I'd lose. I can't fight.

Also, I knew the truth about myself. After all, a person doesn't get called C-C-C-Craig his whole life without earning it!

But Amy stepped back up to Travis and Brad. "Craig is braver than the two of you put together!" she declared, her dark eyes flashing angrily. "And Craig can prove it!"

Huh? I can?

"Go ahead," Amy cried. "Think of a challenge. Try to scare him!"

"No, wait —" I started.

But no one seemed to hear me.

29

"Craig will do anything you want him to!" Amy declared.

I grabbed for her shoulder. I tried to stop her. Too late.

"Go ahead," she insisted. "Think of any challenge. Craig will prove that he isn't afraid of anything!"

A thin smile spread over Travis's lips. His freckles appeared to twinkle. "Want to put some money on that?" he asked slyly.

"No — please," I begged.

"We'll bet you," Amy answered without giving me a chance to say no. "We'll bet any amount of money that you can't frighten Craig — no matter what you try!"

Travis and Brad exchanged glances. Both of them were smiling now.

"Okay," Travis said. "It's a bet. We'll be back."

They hurried away, laughing and talking excitedly.

Amy turned to me. "Easy money — right? Right?"

8

"There's nothing good on TV, and I'm bored with these computer games," Amy groaned. She tossed back her black curly hair. "What do you want to do?"

I shrugged.

It was a gray Saturday afternoon. Raindrops drummed against the window of Amy's den. Out in the backyard, dead leaves rained down from the shivering trees.

"Want to explore the attic?" Amy suggested. "It's dark and creepy up there. My parents have all these boxes filled with old clothes and magazines and stuff."

"I don't think so," I sighed.

I'm secretly scared of attics. I don't like attics or basements. I like to keep to the ground floor, if possible.

"Oh, wait!" Amy jumped up from the carpet. She opened a cabinet against the wall.

Thunder boomed outside. I shivered. I used to be *terrified* of thunderstorms. Now I'm only a little afraid.

Craig, Amy thinks you're really brave, I reminded myself. Don't start whimpering the way you usually do every time you hear a roar of thunder.

If people think you're brave, you *are* brave.

That's what I told myself all week.

But every time I ran into Travis or Brad at school, I wanted to turn and run away.

They know the truth about me, I decided. And they are hatching a plan, a horrible plan to embarrass me and show everyone what a wimp I am.

And *why* are they hatching a plan to terrify me?

Because my new friend Amy challenged them to do it.

I liked Amy. She was a lot of fun to talk to and hang out with.

I wondered if she'd still like me if she found out that I'm not a superhero. That I'm actually a skinny little guy who's afraid of snakes and spiders and thunder and the dark — and a lot of other things.

"Let's watch one of these." Amy spun away from the cabinet with an armful of videos. "My dad rented these last night. I forgot all about them."

"What did he rent?" I asked.

She dropped down beside me on the green leather couch and dumped the videos in my lap. "Check them out. This is perfect," she said. "I'll nuke some popcorn in the microwave, and we'll watch a good, scary movie."

I gulped. "Scary?"

She pulled a box out of the stack. "This one," she said.

I gazed down at the box. It showed two teenage boys and two teenage girls screaming in horror. *Killer Daycamp.* That was the name of the movie.

I remembered the commercials for it on TV. I had to hide my eyes because the commercials were too gory.

"Uh . . . I think I've seen this one," I lied.

"Well, don't give away the creepy parts," Amy replied. She pulled the tape from the box. "You probably *love* scary movies, don't you? How many times have you seen *Killer Daycamp*?"

"Uh . . . only once," I said, swallowing hard.

"I'll make the popcorn, then we'll start it," she said. She jumped up from the couch.

"Maybe one of these other movies is better," I said. I shuffled through the boxes: *Killer Daycamp II . . . Killer Daycamp III: The Revenge . . .*

"I can't believe my parents are into this stuff," Amy said. "They *love* anything with blood and gore."

"Uh . . . me too." Another lie from Craig the superhero.

33

The truth is, scary movies make me shake like a baby. And sometimes I start to scream.

I took a deep breath. Be brave, Craig, I ordered myself. This is the *new* you — remember?

You're a hero.

You're fearless.

A few minutes later, the two of us sat on the couch with bowls of popcorn in our laps, staring at the TV screen.

I did okay for about ten minutes or so. But then the crazed killer jumped out of the woods, swinging his hatchet.

I grabbed the arm of the couch — and opened my mouth in a shrill, bloodcurdling scream.

My heart leaping in my chest, I turned to Amy and found her staring at me, studying me.

She knows, I realized sadly.

Now she knows the truth about me.

Amy stared hard at me. I waited for her to call me a Fraidy Cat and tell me how disappointed she felt.

But instead, her dark eyes flashed and a smile spread over her face. "You're right, Craig," she said.

"Huh? Right?" I choked out.

She nodded. "These movies *are* more fun if you scream along with them!"

My head spun. I don't believe this, I thought. She thinks my scream was *cool*.

We turned back to the movie. The crazed killer stood in the middle of the daycampers' campfire, swinging his hatchet, slicing and dicing.

I let out another terrified scream.

Amy screamed too.

Not a very powerful scream. I guessed she didn't have as much practice as me.

She tilted back her head and screamed again. Much better this time.

We watched the movie and screamed our heads off. It was kind of fun — except that *my* screams were real.

About halfway through the movie, there were very few daycampers left. The crazed hatchet guy burst into the arts-and-crafts cabin. Campers looked up in horror from the beaded key chains they were making.

I opened my mouth to scream.

But a knock on the door cut me off after a tiny squeak.

Amy paused the movie. We both made our way to the front door. "Who's there?" Amy called out.

"Open up!" a boy demanded. "We know you're in there, C-C-C-Craig!"

recognized Travis's voice. He called me C-C-C-Craig.

How did he find out?

Amy flashed me a puzzled glance. Then she pulled open the door.

Travis, Brad, and three other guys stampeded in, shaking off rain. Amy made them wipe their shoes on the floor mat.

Brad pushed back his spiky black hair and grinned at me, a truly evil grin.

I still had the popcorn bowl in my hand. Travis grabbed a handful and stuffed it into his mouth.

"Hi, C-C-C-Craig," David, a chubby, red-haired boy from my class, said. Frankie and Gus, the other two boys, giggled.

My stomach churned. I suddenly felt cold all over.

"Wh-why are you calling me that?" I demanded angrily. (As if I didn't know.)

"My cousin Pam goes to your old school," Travis replied. Popcorn kernels dribbled out of his mouth, onto his chin. He grabbed another handful from my bowl.

I shoved the bowl into his hands. "So? What about her?" I asked, trying to sound tough.

Travis chewed for a while. "She told me about you," he said finally. "She told me *all* about you, C-C-C-Craig. She said you were always scared of your own shadow."

I stared at him. I didn't know what to say.

"She told me you screamed your head off and ran away from a chipmunk last year," Travis said, snickering.

Yes. That was true. But it was a *very big* chipmunk.

"That's a lie," I said.

"It's all a big lie!" Amy chimed in. She glared at Travis and his friends. "None of it is true. You're making it all up because you're jealous of Craig."

Brad turned to me. "Is it true?" he demanded. "Is it true that the kids at your old school called you C-C-C-Craig?"

Amy stared at me. The five guys stared at me.

I took a deep breath. "Of *course* it isn't true," I told them. I shook my head. "Why would someone make up such a dumb story? I don't get it."

Brad's evil grin grew wider. His dark eyes gleamed. "Well . . . we'll see," he said softly.

"We'll see who is telling the truth," Travis added. He set the empty popcorn bowl on a table. "We brought a little test for you, Craig."

Uh-oh.

Lightning flashed in the window. I gritted my teeth and waited for the boom of thunder that followed.

"Test?" I asked. I didn't realize I was backing up, backing away from them. I didn't realize it until I backed into the living room couch and nearly fell over.

They followed me into the living room. Amy eyed them suspiciously. "What kind of test?" she demanded.

"David has it," Travis announced. He turned to his friend.

"I kept it dry, under my jacket," David said. He reached under his jacket — and pulled out a tall glass jar.

"Wh-what is it?" I stammered.

David handed the jar to Travis. Travis raised it in front of my face.

And I let out a horrified gasp.

piders.

Ugly, black hairy-legged spiders. Dozens of them. Crawling all over each other.

Travis pushed the jar against my nose. The spiders blurred into a wriggling pile of black furry bodies and legs.

Amy grabbed the jar away and inspected it. "Where did you find these?" she snapped at Travis. "In your bed?"

The boys all laughed.

I couldn't laugh. I felt like choking. Or fainting. I'm scared of bugs — and spiders are my worst nightmare.

"You told us to bring Craig a challenge," Brad said to Amy. "So, here it is."

I couldn't take my eyes off the strange, hairy

black spiders scrabbling over each other, an end-
less wrestling match.

Do they bite? I wondered. Do they pinch? Are
they poisonous?

"What do I have to do?" I choked out, trying not
to sound frightened. But my voice came out tiny
and weak.

"It's simple," Travis replied. "Just keep your
hand in the jar for five minutes."

Huh?

"No problem!" Amy sneered. "Craig will keep
his hand in there all day! He's not afraid of spiders!"

Amy, please — shut up! I thought.

I stared at the spiders. Then I gazed up at
Travis. "Am I allowed to wear gloves?" I asked.

They all burst out laughing. Amy too.

They thought I was joking.

I can't do this, I realized. I'll *die.*

"How much are we betting?" Amy demanded.

"How about a million dollars?" David suggested.

Everyone laughed again.

"I don't have a million dollars," Amy replied.
"Let's make a real bet, guys. I can't wait to take
your money."

"How about thirty dollars?" Brad suggested.

I gazed into the jar. The black spiders climbed
and wrestled. Were they *biting* each other?

Amy and I are going to lose thirty dollars, I thought miserably.

No way we can win. There's no way I can do this.

I tapped her shoulder. I tried to stop her. But she quickly agreed to the bet. "Okay. Thirty dollars. But this is too easy. Why didn't you think of something hard?"

Amy — please shut up! I thought again. I was gritting my teeth so hard, my jaw ached.

How can I get out of this? I wondered. *Should I just run out the front door and never come back?*

Should I tell them the truth? That I really am C-C-C-Craig?

No. No way, I decided.

I can't let Amy down. I can't let myself down.

If I don't try this, I'll be C-C-C-Craig for the rest of my life.

Travis slid open the metal top of the jar. He turned to his friends. "Who has a watch?"

"I do," Brad replied, holding his wrist close to his face. "I'll keep time."

Travis raised the jar to me. "Five minutes," he said, his expression turning solemn.

I gazed into the jar. "Is that Eastern Standard Time?" I joked.

Travis nodded. "Five minutes in the jar." The boys clustered tight around me, eager to have a good view.

Amy pushed her way into the middle. She flashed me a thumbs-up.

Brad had his eyes on his watch. "Ready. Set. *Go!*"

I took a deep breath. My hand was trembling so hard I wasn't sure I could slide it into the jar.

The glass felt cool against the back of my hand. Shutting my eyes, I plunged my hand down . . . down into the jar.

I was okay for a few seconds.

But then I felt a prickling sensation on the back of my hand. I opened my eyes and saw spiders crawling over my skin.

A moan escaped my throat. I tried to stop it, but I couldn't. I forced a smile to my face to cover it up.

I could feel sweat dripping down my forehead. Could the others see it?

They all had their eyes on my hand in the jar.

Spiders prickled my palm. I felt a few of them drag their hairy, dry bodies over my wrist.

"Thirty seconds," Brad announced.

It felt like thirty years!

At least a dozen spiders clung to my hand now. My arm began to itch. My chest itched. My whole body prickled and itched.

I kept the smile frozen on my face. But I couldn't breathe. I couldn't move.

"One minute," Brad called out.

"Four minutes to go," Travis said, leaning his head closer, grinning as he stared into the jar.

I can't do it, I realized.

Enough.

I can't take anymore.

I lose. I lose the bet. I lose everything.

Spiders danced over the back of my palm. Sharp legs pinched my wrist. Two of them were scuttling up my arm!

That's all. Good-bye, I decided.

I jerked my hand up. Raised it quickly to pull it from the jar.

But I couldn't remove it.

My hand was stuck — stuck inside the jar.

12

I wriggled my hand. I made a tight fist.

I tried to squeeze it tighter, smaller, so it would slide out of the jar.

But it wouldn't budge.

My hand was stuck.

"Two minutes," Brad announced.

"What are you doing?" Travis demanded. "Why are you moving your hand like that?"

"Are they biting you?" Amy asked.

I nodded. "Y-yes. They're . . . biting," I choked out in a hoarse whisper.

"Do you see?" Amy declared to the others. "See how brave Craig is? The spiders are biting him like crazy — and he still keeps his hand in the jar!"

Not if I could help it, I thought bitterly.

I squirmed and struggled to pull my hand out. But it was really stuck.

"Ow!" I let out a cry as a spider bit my thumb.

*I've GOT to get my hand out! Oh, please —
I'll do anything! Please let me slide my hand
out!*

"They're really biting him," Amy declared. "Is
he brave or what?"

Please shut up! I thought, gritting my teeth.
Please — just shut up!

My whole body itched and throbbed. I gritted
my teeth. I couldn't breathe.

Spiders inched up and down both sides of my
hand and around my wrist.

Another sharp pain, another bite, this time on
the back of my wrist.

If only I could pull my hand out, I thought.

I'm going to faint. I'm dizzy. The room is spinning.

This is it. I can't take the itching. The bites . . .
the bites . . .

I'm going to pass out.

"Five minutes are up!" Brad called out.

Travis let out a disappointed groan. "Guess you
win," he muttered, shaking his head.

Brad and the three other guys muttered to each
other, making disappointed sounds.

Amy shot both hands up over her head and
opened her mouth in a cheer of victory. "We win!"
she cried. "We win! We win thirty bucks!"

She turned to me. "Okay, Craig. Time is up. You
can take your hand out."

46

I swallowed. My mouth felt as dry as dust. My heart thudded so hard, I couldn't speak.

What happens when they find out my hand is stuck in the jar? I wondered.

Will that cancel the bet? Will I have to do it all over again?

"Uh . . . that's okay," I said weakly. "I'll keep it in a while longer."

"Huh?" Travis gasped.

They all stared at me, then down at the spiders swarming over my hand.

"Is he crazy?" David muttered.

"You see?" Amy cried, bumping Travis hard, sending him stumbling back. "You see? You think Craig is a wimp? Five minutes isn't enough time for him. He wants to keep it in for another five! That's how brave he is!"

"Amy, please —" I croaked.

Why can't she keep her big mouth shut?

"Pay up, guys," Amy demanded, holding out her hand. "Come on. Let's see it. Thirty bucks."

Her expression changed. "Oh. Wait. Forget the thirty," she said. "How about double or nothing?"

"Amy, *please* —" I begged. But my voice came out so weak no one heard me.

"Yeah. Double or nothing," Travis agreed quickly.

Spiders stampeded over the back of my hand. I felt another bite. My whole hand throbbed with pain.

I'm going to die! I realized. I'm going to die right now in this room!

"Think of something harder next time," Amy told them. "Think of something scary." She laughed. "Craig and I don't like taking your money so easily!"

"Please —" I begged.

"Don't worry. We won't go easy on him next time," Travis promised.

"Don't worry. Next time, we'll prove that he's C-C-C-Craig," Brad agreed.

Amy opened the front door, and the five guys tromped out into the rain.

Amy closed the door and turned back to me with a pleased grin. "Easy money, huh?"

"*Help me . . .*" I gasped. I waved the jar at her. "Help me . . . get this off."

She squinted down at the jar. "It's stuck?"

I nodded.

She grabbed the sides and tugged with both hands. The jar made a loud *POP* as it finally came off.

"Oh, wow," I moaned.

"Your hand — it's kind of red," Amy said. She made a disgusted face. "Yuck. It's kind of *swollen* too. No wonder it got stuck."

I took several deep breaths. The itching and throbbing just wouldn't quit.

"That must really hurt," Amy said fretfully.

"Hey — no big deal," I replied.

I'll never be able to use it again, I told myself. *I'll never stop itching. I'll have nightmares about hairy black spiders crawling all over me for the rest of my life.*

I flicked several spiders off my hand, back into the jar.

"You really are brave," Amy murmured. "That hand is totally gross."

Thanks a bunch.

"I've had worse," I lied. "I guess I'd better get home. Put some cream on it or something."

"I guess," she replied. "It looks really *sick.*"

I said good-bye and hurried out into the rain. It was pouring, but I didn't care. The cold raindrops felt soothing on my throbbing, itching hand.

As soon as I got home, I ran into the bathroom. I filled the sink with cold water and soaked my hand until it stopped burning. Then I rubbed every cream I could find in the medicine chest on it.

Finally, it felt a little better, a little more normal.

But I didn't.

I gazed at the frightened expression on my reflection in the mirror and thought about Travis and Brad and their grinning friends.

What will they have in store for me next? I wondered.

How long can I pretend to be brave?

13

"I just keep thinking about how you rescued that baby," Amy said. "That was so awesome!"

"Yeah. Whatever," I replied.

It was a week later, a clear, cold Saturday night. Amy's parents were out for the night. So we were hanging out at her house again.

"You probably want to watch more of those scary videos," Amy said. She wore an oversized black sweater over a blue sweater and kept tugging the sleeves down. "But we can't. My dad took them back to the rental store."

"Too bad," I replied. Secretly, I wanted to jump up and down for joy. I couldn't take another trip to *Killer Daycamp*. The sequels were supposed to be even more gross than the first one!

A tap on the window nearly made me jump out of my skin.

Travis and his friends?

No. A pebble or a leaf or something, blown against the glass.

Travis had been hinting all week that he had something really terrifying planned for me. "Double or nothing," he said, grinning. "And *you* are going to end up with nothing."

I begged him to give me a hint.

He only laughed and rubbed his hands together like an evil cartoon villain.

"Do you like Ping-Pong?" Amy asked.

I nodded. "Yeah. I won the Ping-Pong championship at camp last summer."

Her dark eyes flashed. "Really?"

No. Not really. Actually, my *team* won the championship. I was the worst player on the team.

"Too bad you don't have a table," I said. "I'd give you a few lessons."

She giggled. "We *do* have a table." She grabbed my hand. "Come on. It's in the basement. Maybe I'll give *you* a few lessons. I have a really cool spin serve."

A spin serve? What's that? Whenever I served, the ball usually dove right for the net.

I stopped at the top of the basement stairs and Amy clicked on the ceiling light. The stairs were dark and steep.

"Dad built a whole rec room down there," Amy said. "The only problem is, the dryer steams up the whole basement."

I grabbed the railing and started down the steps. The wooden stairs creaked under my shoes.

I was halfway down when the light flickered out.

I stopped. And peered down into total blackness.

Amy bumped me from behind. I grabbed the railing to keep from falling the rest of the way.

"That light — it's always going out," Amy said. "I think it's got a short or something."

You probably guessed that I'm afraid of the dark.

I'm not afraid of the dark in places that I know really well. I mean, I don't need a night-light in my bedroom at night.

But I'd never been in Amy's basement. And standing here on these creaky stairs, unable to see my own sneakers, I started to shake.

"Well? Go on down," Amy ordered. "Why did you stop?"

I cleared my throat. My hand gripped the rail tightly. "Well . . . it's so dark . . . ," I murmured.

Amy laughed. "You're not afraid of the dark — are you, Craig?"

I forced a laugh. "Of course not." My voice cracked.

"Well — keep going," Amy insisted. She gave

my shoulder a gentle push that almost sent me sprawling.

"I'm . . . w-w-well . . . ," I stammered. "I'm not afraid of the dark. But — I'm afraid of *basements.*"

Amy uttered a startled cry. "Huh? Basements? You mean — there really is something you're afraid of?"

My throat felt tight, blocked. As if I had swallowed a whole walnut. I cleared my throat again. "Yeah. Basements," I choked out.

"Why?" Amy demanded.

"When I was little . . . ," I started. *Think fast, Craig. Make up something good, something she'll believe.*

"When I was little, my mom brought me down to the basement. She was ironing or cleaning up or something. I don't remember what she was doing. But I remember everything else so clearly," I said.

Think fast, Craig. What happened? What scared you?

"What happened?" Amy asked.

Good question.

"Uh . . . the phone rang upstairs," I continued. "Mom ran up to answer it. She forgot all about me. She left me down there."

"How old were you?" Amy asked.

"Uh . . . I don't know. I was too young to count," I replied. "But I couldn't walk yet, I remember. I could only sit up. And . . . and . . ."

And what? Think of something, Craig.

"This is hard for you to talk about," Amy said softly.

"Uh . . . yeah," I replied. "Because these mice came out of their holes. I don't know. Maybe they were mice. Maybe they were rats. But I was all alone down there. And they came out of their holes and . . ."

"How awful!" Amy declared. "You must have been terrified. What did they do?"

What did they do? What did they do? Did they pluck out my eyes? No. Did they bite my little legs? No.

"They just stared at me," I said. "I'll never forget their evil stares, their glowing red eyes." I sighed. "It seemed like hours. The mice stood there in a line, staring, staring, staring. I've been afraid of basements ever since."

Now Amy knows the truth about me, I thought, peering down into the dark basement. Now she knows I'm really a quivering coward.

"That's the bravest thing I ever heard!" Amy declared.

"Excuse me?" I cried.

"Telling me that story," Amy replied. "Telling that awful story was so brave! It must have been so hard for you."

"Well . . . you know —"

A loud buzz interrupted me. The doorbell. The front doorbell.

54

Saved by the bell, I thought.

Wrong.

"I know who that is," Amy said. She turned and ran back up the stairs.

I eagerly followed her. "Who is it?"

"Travis and Brad and the others," Amy replied, striding to the front door.

"Huh?"

Amy turned back to me. "I forgot to tell you. They said they were coming over tonight to challenge you again."

"Oh, wow," I murmured, feeling a chill tighten the back of my neck. Then I quickly added, "Why don't they just give up? No way they can scare me."

"I know," Amy agreed. "This is easy money!"

"Uh . . . did they tell you what the challenge is?" I asked, trying to sound as if I didn't really care.

She nodded. "They said they're bringing a really big, poisonous snake. And they want you to kiss it on the mouth. No problem — right?"

My mouth dropped open.

Kiss a snake? Kiss a *poisonous* snake?

I swallowed hard and started to admit to Amy that there was *no way* I would ever *touch* a snake, let alone *kiss* one.

But before I could get a word out, I heard desperate cries and moans from outside.

And then Brad's frightened voice from the other side of the door: "Help us! Please — help!"

14

my and I exchanged troubled glances. Then she grabbed the door and yanked it open.

Brad burst into the room, his eyes wide with horror. "Help us!" he cried. "Hurry!"

I saw David with Gus and Frankie behind him. And then I saw Travis.

Travis had both hands pressed over his eyes, as if blindfolding himself. Bright-red blood poured down his face.

"Are your parents home? We've got to get help!" David wailed.

"No! What happened?" Amy gasped.

"We — we had a big snake," Brad stammered, breathing hard. "It got away. Travis — he chased after it. He was running and . . . and he tripped and fell."

"Travis poked his eye out!" David cried.

"Ohhhhh." Travis uttered a low groan.

Slowly, he lowered his right hand. Opened it.

And I gaped at the big, watery eyeball in his blood-smeared palm.

"Help me," Travis groaned. "Ohhhh, it hurts. It hurts so much!"

"Call a doctor!" David cried. "Call an ambulance!"

"Help . . . ohhh . . . help . . . ," Travis moaned.

I felt my stomach lurch. I clapped a hand over my mouth to keep my dinner from coming up.

Amy let out a sick cry.

I stared at the wet, veiny eyeball. I couldn't stop staring at it.

"It hurts . . . ," Travis moaned again. "Please . . . do something."

I stared at the eyeball for another second.

And then I rushed forward. Plucked the eyeball from Travis's hand.

And popped it into my mouth.

15

Amy shrieked in horror.

Brad let out a startled cry. David and the others gasped.

I turned to Travis and rolled the eyeball slowly from side to side in my mouth.

Travis started to laugh. He lowered his other hand from over his eyes.

I poked the eyeball through my lips.

Everyone was laughing now.

I spit the eyeball into my hand and tossed it to Travis. "Very real-looking," I said. "I saw these plastic eyes in the same card store you did. A Halloween display — right?"

"Right." Brad sighed.

Travis turned to Amy. "Got any paper towels? I have to wipe this fake blood off. It's dripping all over."

Amy ran to the kitchen and returned with a wad of paper towels. "Craig wasn't scared for a second," she told Travis. "Was that your second challenge? You'll have to do a lot better than that."

She stuck out her hand. "You owe us sixty bucks, guys. Pay up."

Travis tossed the plastic eyeball to her. It hit her on the shoulder and bounced to the floor.

"That wasn't our dare," Brad insisted. "It was just a joke. We just wanted to see C-C-C-Craig lose his dinner."

"Well, he didn't — did he!" Amy sneered.

I shuddered. If I hadn't seen those eyeballs in the store window yesterday, my dinner would have been all over Amy's living room carpet.

How lucky could I get?

David picked up the eyeball and tossed it to Gus, who tossed it to Frankie. They started a game of eyeball catch across the living room.

Travis mopped the red liquid off his face. He balled up the paper towels and tossed them at me. "Think fast!"

David heaved the eyeball. It bounced off a lamp. The lamp shook but didn't fall.

"Cut it out, guys!" Amy ordered. "My parents will be home any minute." She turned to Travis. "You never even *had* a snake — did you!"

He shook his head. "No. Snakes aren't scary enough. Not for the superhero here." He patted my shoulder. "C-C-Captain C-C-C-Craig," he said.

"You guys are total losers," Amy told them, shaking her head. "You're not clever enough to scare Craig. No way you can win the bet."

"Oh, yeah?" Brad shot back. "You might as well pay us the sixty dollars now, Amy."

"That's right," Travis agreed. "Craig will *never* do what we have planned for him next."

"Huh? What's that?" I asked weakly.

A sly grin spread over Travis's freckled face. "You know my dad owns a funeral parlor," he said quietly.

"So?" Amy snapped.

Travis's grin grew wider. "So . . . use your imagination."

At lunch hour on Monday afternoon, Amy and I walked out of class. We turned the corner — and heard loud, angry voices. Then the crash of a locker door.

I stopped when I saw Brad across the hall. "Grant — get your paws off me!" he shrieked.

His older brother had Brad by the front of the shirt. Grant lifted Brad off the floor and slammed his back into the tile wall.

"Get out of my face!" Brad shrieked furiously.

Grant laughed. "Make me!"

He lowered his shoulder and bumped Brad hard in the chest, sending him sprawling against the wall again. Then he jerked Brad away from the wall, yanked open the locker, and started to stuff Brad inside.

"He can't do that to Brad," Amy said angrily. She gave me a push. "Go teach Grant a lesson."

"Excuse me?" I took a step back.

"Go stand up to Grant," Amy insisted. "You're the only one who can do it. Brad is terrified of his brother. But you're not afraid of anything. Go ahead!"

I gulped. "But . . . but . . . it wouldn't be right."

Amy narrowed her dark eyes at me.

"Brad has to fight his own battles," I said. "Besides, it's a family thing."

"Oh, go ahead," Amy replied. She gave me another shove, into the center of the hall. "You know you're not afraid of Grant. Give Brad a break. Look what Grant is doing to him!"

Once again, Grant had shoved his brother into the locker. He held him inside with a fist on his chest. "Say please," Grant ordered.

"Okay. Please," Brad whimpered.

"Say pretty please," Grant insisted.

"Pretty please," Brad repeated. "Ow! You're hurting me!"

Laughing, very pleased with himself, Grant shoved his fist harder into Brad's stomach. Then he spun from the locker and strode away, heading toward Amy and me.

"Go ahead — get him!" Amy urged. She shoved me again.

"No. Really —" I tried to back away.

But I stumbled into Grant.

"Hey!" He cried out as he tripped over my shoe.

His hands shot out as he fell forward, fell on his face.

"Whoa!" I stumbled over his outstretched arm — fell — and landed on his back.

"Yaaay! Way to go! Way to go, Craig!" Amy cheered.

I glanced up to see a crowd of kids laughing and cheering.

"Get off me!" Grant growled. His face was bright red. I think he was totally embarrassed.

He tossed me off and climbed to his feet.

"Way to go, Craig!" Amy cheered.

Kids clapped and hooted.

"What's up?" I heard a girl ask.

"Craig punched out Grant!" a boy replied.

"Craig wasted Brad's big brother."

"He wrecked him!"

Grant snarled at me again and stomped off furiously, swinging his fists at his sides.

I sat stunned on the floor. Two hands reached down to help pull me up. Brad's hands.

He studied me. "You okay?"

I nodded. "Yeah. I guess."

"I don't believe you did that!" Brad exclaimed. "I never saw anyone stand up to Grant. Wow. You really *are* brave!"

"No, listen —" I started.

"That was awesome!" Brad declared. "Awesome!" He slapped me a high five.

"But it was an accident," I told him. "I didn't mean to trip him. Amy pushed me and —"

"You don't have to be modest," Brad said. "I saw the whole thing, Craig. You handled him. You *handled* him!"

Amy slapped me on the back, so hard I nearly choked. "You handled him! Wow. You *mangled* him! That's the bravest thing I ever saw!"

So I felt pretty good about myself for the rest of the afternoon.

I mean, I knew the whole thing had been an accident. A lucky accident.

But everyone else in school believed that I took down Brad's big bully of a brother. Everyone believed I was the bravest thing on two legs.

Maybe I *am* kind of brave, I told myself.

I was sitting in class, not hearing a word anyone said. Thinking about all that had happened to me since I moved to Middle Valley.

Maybe it isn't what a person thinks or feels that makes him brave, I thought. Maybe it's what he *does*.

If I do brave things — even if I don't *feel* brave — maybe that makes me brave.

See? I almost had myself convinced that I wasn't C-C-C-Craig any longer. I almost had myself convinced that I was a new, brave me.

I was almost convinced — until I walked out of

class after the last bell and heard Travis and Brad talking in the doorway to a supply closet.

Hearing them say my name, I pressed against the wall so they couldn't see me. And I listened.

"You're not going ahead with it — are you, Travis?" Brad asked.

"Of course I am," Travis snickered. "We'll make C-C-C-Craig shake like a leaf."

"But that's going too far!" Brad protested. "That's *too* horrible. You're not really going to try it — are you?"

Travis's reply sent a shiver down my back. He grunted. "Watch me."

17

A few nights later, Amy and I were hunched over my dining room table doing homework. Amy was working on math problems, moving her lips as she added and subtracted.

I was writing an essay about Aaron Burr. Well, actually, I was copying some of it from an encyclopedia.

When the doorbell buzzed, I broke the point of my pencil.

I knew who it was. I could tell by the buzz. It was Travis and Brad, coming to test me, to terrify me.

Take it easy, Craig, I told myself. You're shaking already, and you don't even know what they planned for you.

Pretend you're brave, I instructed myself. If you pretend you're brave, you'll *be* brave.

Big words. Who was I kidding?

Amy followed me to the front door. I pulled it open. Brad stepped in, wearing a blue down jacket and a wool ski hat. "It's pretty cold out there," he explained.

He tugged off the hat and glanced around nervously. "I'm sorry about this, Craig," he murmured, avoiding my eyes. "Really."

"Oh, sure." Amy rolled her eyes. "You're just trying to frighten him, Brad. But it isn't going to work."

"No. I mean it," Brad insisted. "I think Travis went too far this time. I tried to argue with him, but he wouldn't listen. He really wants to win this bet."

Those words sent chills down my back. I could feel my knees start to buckle. I grabbed the back of the couch for support.

Maybe I should concede, I thought. Give up now. Before things get out of control.

"I just wanted to say that I'm sorry in advance," Brad said solemnly, eyes on the floor.

I gulped.

"The only ones who will be sorry are you and Travis and your buddies," Amy insisted. "Because after tonight is over, you'll owe us sixty bucks."

"We'll see," Brad murmured. He motioned to the door. "Get your coats and follow me."

*   *   *

67

We stepped out into a cold, windy October night. Dead leaves swirled in wild circles over the lawns. The nearly bare trees creaked and groaned.

I felt a few cold drops of rain on my forehead. So I zipped my black down parka and pulled the hood up over my head.

We turned the corner, waited for a nearly empty city bus to rumble past, then made our way toward town.

I knew where we were going. Travis had already hinted about it. I remembered the gleeful smirk on his freckled face when he mentioned it.

Sure enough, we crept up behind the low hedge at the back of the parking lot. A yellow spotlight lit up the wooden sign in front of the long, dark-shingled building. The sign read: SHADY REST.

The funeral parlor that Travis's dad owned.

I shivered.

Were there dead bodies in there? Actual corpses?

Of course there are, Craig. I answered my own dumb question. It's a funeral parlor — right?

I shoved my hands deep into my coat pockets. I hoped Amy couldn't see me shivering.

"Hey — here's the superhero!" David greeted me with a slap on the back. Gus and Frankie nodded solemnly.

"Where's Travis?" Amy demanded.

A gust of wind made the long hedge wriggle, like a snake. The wind blew the hood back onto my shoulders. I felt another cold raindrop on my forehead.

"Travis got caught," Brad replied.

"Huh? Caught?" I cried.

Brad nodded. "His parents caught him sneaking out."

"He's going to miss all the fun," David smirked.

Some fun, I thought bitterly.

"But, don't worry, Craig," David continued. "We'll give Travis a full report about how you ran away screaming."

"*You're* the ones who will scream," Amy insisted, "when you have to pay us the bet money!"

I turned and stared at the funeral parlor. It was a plain, one-story, shingled building. But it suddenly looked to me like one of those dark, evil castles in a horror movie.

I pictured rows of black coffins inside. And dead bodies, stretched out on metal tables. And green corpses staggering around, groaning. Blank lifeless eyes rolling around in their decaying heads. Coffin lids pushing up . . . bony hands poking out.

Craig — stop! I ordered myself. Stop imagining!

I swallowed hard and turned to Brad. "What do I have to do?" I asked.

rad and the three other boys stared at me. David started to giggle. Gus and Frankie laughed too. Cruel, cold laughter.

Brad's expression remained solemn. "This wasn't my idea," he murmured.

"Don't pay any attention to them," Amy warned me. "They think they can scare you."

They *are* scaring me, I thought. They're scaring me, and I don't even know *why* yet.

Amy turned to Brad. "Why don't you just give up now? Craig can't be scared by anything."

"We'll see," Brad replied. He pointed to the funeral parlor. "See that back window, Craig?"

I peered over the hedge at the building. Totally dark. All the windows and doors dark. The only light was the spotlight beaming down on the

SHADY REST sign at the front of the empty parking lot.

"See the window I'm pointing to?" Brad repeated.

I nodded.

"That's the window you'll go in," he said.

"Huh? Go *in*?" I gasped. "Go *in*?"

Brad nodded. The other boys laughed.

"Isn't that illegal?" I asked, trying to keep my voice low and steady, trying desperately to sound calm. "Does Travis's dad know about this?"

"Of course not," Brad replied.

David shook his head. "If Travis's dad knew, he'd *bury* us all!"

Gus and Frankie thought that was a riot. They burst out laughing and slapped David high fives.

"Ssshhh, quiet, guys," Brad warned. "We don't want to get caught *before* Craig goes inside."

"Just tell him what he has to do," Amy said impatiently. "He'll do it. You'll pay us the money. And then we can get out of here. It's cold!"

"It's real simple," Brad said, putting a hand on the shoulder of my coat. He pointed again to the narrow window at the back of the building.

"Craig, you slide the window up," Brad instructed. "You climb inside. You open up the first coffin you find. And you lie down inside it."

"But — but —" I gasped.

"That's *all*?" Amy cried. "That's *all* he has to

do? This is too easy! You guys are *giving* your money away!"

"Amy, please —" I started to beg.

"H-how —" I stammered. "How?"

"Can't you think of anything challenging?" Amy cried to Brad. "Can't you think of something a little bit scary?"

"How will you know if I do it?" I finally choked out.

"Easy," Brad replied. "We'll be watching. We'll be watching your every move from that back window."

"But what if we get caught?" I demanded.

"We won't," Brad replied. "There's no one around, Craig. Only dead people."

"You're not afraid of dead people — are you, Craig?" David asked, grinning.

Yes, I answered to myself. *Yes, of course I am.*

I've never seen a dead person before.

I've never even seen a *coffin* before. Let alone climbed into one.

A blast of wind made the hedge shiver. Cold raindrops splashed my forehead. Shivering, I pulled the hood back over my hair.

"Go do it, Craig," Amy urged. "Let's get it over with. These guys are a waste of time."

I gazed across the dark parking lot. Could I do it? Could I sneak into the funeral parlor and lie down in a coffin?

As I huddled behind the hedge, the building seemed a mile away.

My legs are shaking too hard, I told myself. I can't even walk that far.

Just tell them the truth, Craig, I thought. Tell them you're the biggest chicken that ever clucked. Tell them it's all a big mistake. You're not brave. You've never been brave.

Amy will be upset. But she'll get over it . . . in a year or two.

But then there's the sixty-dollar bet. I can't pay it. Where will I get that kind of money?

You have no choice, Craig. You have to do it.

"Okay. Here goes," I said. I pulled the hood down over my forehead. Leaning into the wind, I pushed through a split in the hedge and stepped into the parking lot.

I was halfway across the lot when a blinding, bright light swept over me.

Caught!

19

I froze as the light rolled over me.

Shielding my eyes, I turned to the street. And saw a dark van pulling into the driveway to the funeral parlor.

My heart pounding, I staggered back. Turned. And dove for the safety of the hedge.

"Who's that?" I asked Brad breathlessly.

He shrugged.

We all ducked low behind the shivering hedge. And watched as two white-uniformed men climbed out of the van.

They pulled open the back door. Then, struggling and groaning, they lifted out a long black plastic bag.

A body bag?

Was there a body inside the bag?

We watched in silence as they vanished around

the other side of the building, carrying their heavy load.

"A late delivery," Amy whispered.

I saw Brad shiver.

Gus and Frankie got very quiet.

I realized I'd been holding my breath the whole time. My lungs ached. They felt about to burst. I let the air out in a long whoosh.

"Did you see? I was almost caught," I murmured. "That was a close call."

"Do you want to quit?" David demanded. "Want to give up?"

"Too scared to go in, C-C-C-Craig?" Gus chimed in.

"Of course he isn't scared!" Amy answered for me. "He's going in — as soon as they leave."

I shoved my hands deeper into my parka pockets. I tried to hide my face under the hood. I didn't want anyone to see how terrified I was.

The lights flashed on in the side windows of the funeral parlor. An eerie green light filled the curtained windows.

A minute or so later, the light went out. The two men returned to the van. They slammed the back door shut. Climbed into the front. And drove away.

I turned and saw everyone staring at me.

"I'm going," I murmured.

Once again, I squeezed through the opening in the hedge. And started to cross the parking lot.

The others followed close behind. Our shoes scraped the damp pavement.

Behind the building, bare trees swayed and shook, as if waving us away.

A narrow strip of grass led to the back of the funeral parlor. My shoes sank into the wet ground, making a soft *SQUISH* with every step.

The blood pulsed at my temples as I reached the back window. I tried to peer through the glass, but curtains blocked the view. Besides, it was too dark inside to see anything.

"Go ahead. Open the window," Brad urged. His voice came out shrill and breathless. He sounded frightened too.

Raindrops had spattered the windowpane. I reached both hands to the wooden frame. And pushed.

The window slid up easily. A gust of wind made the curtains billow, like two filmy ghosts.

I leaned over the window ledge and peered inside.

Where was the dead body those guys brought in?

I couldn't see a thing.

A sharp, sour smell made me hold my breath. "What stinks?" I blurted out.

"Corpses," David replied, his back pressed against the shingled wall. "Decaying, rotting corpses."

"Don't listen to him. It's formaldehyde," Amy

said. "You know. The stuff they use to embalm the corpses."

"Yuck." I took a deep breath through my mouth. The sour smell made my stomach churn.

"Do you want to quit?" Brad asked. I felt his hand on the shoulder of my parka. "Are you afraid? Want to give up? Just say the word."

"No way!" Amy cried. "Craig doesn't *know* the word *afraid*. He's going in." She turned to me. "Want a boost?"

"No," I replied quickly. I raised both hands to the window ledge. "I'll just climb in."

I leaned into the open window. The silky curtains billowed against my face. I started to hoist myself up.

"Remember — the first coffin you see," Brad reminded. "Open it up and climb in."

"We'll be watching," David added.

"Wish I brought my camera," Gus chimed in. "I've never taken a picture of a guy screaming his head off."

"Shut up, Gus," Amy snapped. She said something else, but I didn't hear her.

I dropped inside the funeral parlor with a *THUD*, landing on my hands and knees.

I waited a few seconds to catch my breath. Then I climbed slowly to my feet.

I jumped as the window curtains, blown by the wind, brushed against my back. The curtains wrapped around me, as if trying to hold me back.

I tore them away, blinking, struggling to see in the blackness.

"Can I turn on a light?" I called to the window. "I can't see a thing."

"No. No lights," Brad whispered. "Someone might see. Here." He clicked on a flashlight, held it up to the open window, and sent a dim beam of light darting over the floor.

"Big help," I muttered to myself.

I took a few steps into the room — tripped over something on the floor — fell forward — and landed on top of it.

A body!

20

"Oh, nooooo!" I opened my mouth in a moan of horror.

I rolled off it. Scrambled to my feet.

No. Please — no!

I gazed down. Not a body. Some kind of duffel bag. A supply bag maybe.

I froze, struggling to catch my breath.

"What's wrong, C-C-C-Craig?" David's mocking voice snapped me into action.

"Nothing," I called back to them. "No problem." I hoped they didn't notice how my voice was shaking.

The circle of light from Brad's flashlight bounced around at my feet. One of the other boys clicked on another flashlight. So now, two circles of light swirled around like mini-spotlights over the floor.

I squinted around the room. A long room with a

79

low ceiling just a foot or two over my head. I saw two metal tables side by side. One of them stood bare. The other was covered by a sheet.

A desk cluttered with papers. A row of filing cabinets against one wall. Coils and tubes. Equipment that looked as if it belonged in a hospital.

And then . . .

. . . coffins.

A long row of dark wood coffins, shiny in the light from the darting flashlights. Coffins resting on low tables.

"Oh, wow," I murmured. My mouth dropped open.

I shielded my eyes as one of the flashlight beams rolled onto my face. "Cut it out!" I called angrily to the window.

"The first coffin," Brad instructed. "Go to the first coffin."

I turned and saw him pointing with the flashlight.

"He's wimping out," I heard Frankie say. "Step back, guys. Give him room to run."

"He's not running," Amy said sharply. "Go get 'em, Craig!" she shouted. "This is easy money!"

Easy for *her*, maybe.

I stared from coffin to coffin. Could I really climb in one?

What did it feel like? I wondered. What did it *smell* like?

My heart pounding, I turned back to the window. "Do I have to pull the lid closed over me?" I asked, staring into the twin circles of light.

"Just climb in," Brad replied impatiently. "Are you going to do it or not, Craig? It's getting cold out here."

"Of course he's going to do it," Amy answered for me again.

I turned and walked slowly up to the first coffin. The two beams of light flashed onto the green wall above it. The coffin lid was closed.

"Go, Craig! Go, Craig!" Amy chanted, urging me on.

"What is he waiting for?" David whispered.

I lowered my hands to the coffin lid. The wood felt cool and smooth. My heart pounded so hard I could barely breathe.

Push it up and jump in, Craig, I told myself.

Don't even think about it — just do it.

It's no big deal. No big deal at all. A coffin is just a big wooden box.

It's no different from lying down on a bed.

My hands left cold, wet spots on the shiny wood. The circles of light danced on the wall.

I gripped the lid. Took a deep breath.

Pushed with all my strength.

The coffin lid slid open. I gazed inside — and started to scream.

21

Dark eyes stared up at me — glassy, blank eyes.

I saw dark lips, frozen in a sick, unnatural smile. One jagged tooth poked out over the bottom lip.

The face.

I couldn't really see the face clearly. It was hidden in deep shadow.

But I could see deep scars across its forehead and cheeks.

And I could see the dark form of the body. Two arms crossed over the chest.

Lying still . . . so still.

Was I still screaming — or had I stopped? My shrill wail still rang in my ears.

"Craig — what's wrong?" Amy's voice rose over the sound. "What is it?"

"A — a corpse," I stammered, pointing with a trembling finger into the coffin.

"I told you he'd scream," I heard Gus say.

I heard the other boys snickering.

"Big surprise. A corpse in a funeral home!"

They laughed again.

"It isn't funny," I gasped. "It's a dead body."

My stomach churned. My throat tightened so hard, my breath whistled.

The lights lowered to the floor. I struggled to see the corpse's face.

No. No. Too dark.

"So do you give up?" Brad demanded.

"He can't do it!" Gus declared.

"We win!" David cheered. "We win sixty big ones!"

"No way!" Amy protested. She poked her head through the window. "You can still do it — right, Craig? You can lie down in there? Easy, right?"

"Huh?" I choked out, my voice cracking. "Lie down on top of the corpse?"

"I know you're not afraid," Amy said.

Not afraid? I'm TERRIFIED!

"Do it!" Amy urged.

I turned back to the coffin. Outside the window, the others grew silent. I peered into the darting gray light.

I gripped the side of the coffin.

The sour odor of formaldehyde swirled around me. I suddenly felt sick. My stomach lurched.

I leaned over the coffin.
Can I do it? Can I climb in?
No, I realized.
No. I can't. No way. I just can't.
I let go of the coffin and started to back away.
I heard a groan.
And saw a quick gray blur.
The hand.
The corpse's hand.
It shot up — and grabbed the front of my parka.

22

I opened my mouth to scream — but no sound came out.

The hand tightened its grip.

The other hand grabbed on.

The corpse gave a hard tug, pulling me into the coffin.

"No —" I gasped. I tried to pull back.

The corpse sat up. Gripping my parka. Pulling . . . pulling me in . . .

The glassy eyes glared at me without blinking.

The scars over the cheek and forehead throbbed darkly.

"No . . . no . . ." I gripped the corpse's wrists. Tried to shove the dead hands off.

But the corpse dove forward and wrapped its hands around my shoulders.

It used me to pull itself up. Then to pull me down into the coffin.

"No . . . No . . ." The word escaped my throat in a horrified chant. "No . . ."

The corpse kept pulling. My face was buried in its chest.

I jerked back.

And fell to the floor — taking the corpse with me.

"Ouch!" I cried out in pain as the body landed heavily on top of me.

"Get off! Get off!" I shrieked.

Before I even realized what I was doing, I was wrestling with it. Rolling out from under it. Pushing . . . pushing it away.

But the corpse held on to my arms. Pulled me down on top of it.

We wrestled frantically, rolling over and over.

Groaning and grunting. Tugging at each other.

My chest ached. My head spun.

I shot up both hands. Grabbed the corpse's wiry black hair.

Grabbed the hair — and tugged. Tugged with all my strength.

And pulled its head off!

o. Not its head.

Not a head.

The scars wrinkled. The mouth, with its one overhanging tooth, collapsed.

A mask. A rubber mask.

Swallowing hard, I lowered my gaze — and stared at Travis's scowling face.

Travis? Travis in the coffin?

Of course. Why hadn't I guessed?

We stared at each other, our mouths open, chests heaving up and down, both struggling to catch our breath.

I expected him to jump up. Laugh. Celebrate his victory.

But instead, he shook his head unhappily. "How did you know it was me?" he asked.

Ceiling lights flashed on. Blinking in the bright light, I turned and saw that the others had climbed in through the window.

Brad picked up the ugly, scarred mask and rolled it around on his hand. Amy reached out and helped pull me to my feet.

"How did you know it was me?" Travis demanded again.

"Well . . ." I felt so stunned, I couldn't think.

I had *no idea* it was Travis. I really thought a corpse had come to life!

"You didn't fool Craig for a minute!" Amy's voice broke into my thoughts. "See? You can't scare him. He's too brave and he's too smart."

"I don't get it," Travis murmured, still down on the floor. "I thought you'd turn and run. I thought you'd run out of here screaming and never stop. I really did."

Amy let out a scornful laugh. "That'll be the day!" She turned to the others. "Pay up, losers. Sixty bucks."

"You fought me and pulled off my mask," Travis said. He appeared to be in shock. "How did you know? How?"

I shrugged. I didn't know what to say.

I couldn't tell him the truth. That I was *petrified*. That I nearly *died* of fright.

I've got to stop this crazy game, I told myself. I've got to stop Travis and Brad. And Amy!

But Amy's voice rang out again. "So you dressed

up as a corpse? A phony corpse? That was no big deal," she bragged. "Craig isn't afraid of fake corpses. He isn't afraid of *real* corpses!"

"Oh, yeah?" Travis replied, finally climbing to his feet.

"Craig will climb into a coffin with a real corpse," Amy declared. "No problem!"

Amy — shut up! Shut up! I thought. I balled my hands into tight fists.

Why didn't she ever check with me first? Did she really think I could do *anything*?

Travis narrowed his eyes at me. He brushed a ball of lint off the shoulder of my parka. "Not afraid of real corpses, huh?" he said, studying me.

"Well . . . ," I started.

"Okay. We'll see about that," Travis said.

"No . . . uh . . . ," I stammered.

Travis turned to Amy. "One last bet," he told her. "Craig's final challenge."

I hated the way he said *final*!

"Double or nothing," Travis added. "We'll meet you back here. Real soon."

24

The next night, I paced back and forth in my room and practiced my speech to Amy. "This has to stop. I don't want a final challenge. I can't take one more dare. I really can't take it."

I said the words out loud. I repeated my speech again and again, until I knew every word by heart.

Maybe, I thought, if I tell her the truth, Amy will finally listen to me.

If I stop pretending and let her know the truth about me, I know she'll stop bragging about me. And I can live a normal, peaceful, *safe* life.

I ran through the speech one more time. Then I picked up the phone and punched in Amy's number.

She picked up after the third ring.

"Hi, it's me," I said. My whole body felt tense

and tight. But I didn't care. In a few minutes, I hoped, my nightmare would be over.

"Craig, what did you get for the third math problem?" she asked.

"I don't want to talk about math now," I replied.

"I *never* want to talk about math!" she exclaimed. "But I need help with the third problem."

I sighed and dropped down onto the edge of my bed. "Listen, I have to tell you something," I said.

Silence for a moment.

"Are you okay?" she asked finally. "You sound so . . . serious."

"I need to tell you something," I repeated.

"Okay. Shoot," she replied.

I took a deep breath and started my speech. "I'm not brave," I announced.

"Excuse me?"

"I'm not brave, Amy. I've been terrified ever since I moved to Middle Valley. I —"

"Craig, I saw how brave you are — remember?" Amy interrupted. "I saw you risk your life to rescue that baby in the car. And I saw you climb that tree to save the little boy. And rescue the bird's nest, and —"

"It was all an accident," I insisted. "Please — let me finish."

I took another deep breath. Confessing the truth was hard. But I had to do it.

"You know when Travis said I used to be called C-C-C-Craig? It's true. That's what kids called me at my old school. They called me C-C-C-Craig because I was a total wimp. And I still am, Amy."

Silence at her end of the line. I could hear her breathing. But she didn't say a word.

"All of these dares," I continued. "They're scaring me to death. I can't take it anymore. That's why I'm finally telling you the truth. I want you to call off the bet. Call the whole thing off."

I sighed. "I'm too scared. I really am. Call off the bet. Okay? Okay?"

Silence again at Amy's end.

Finally! I thought. I finally got through to her.

"Craig, you're such a nice person," she said finally.

"Excuse me? Nice?"

"You're the nicest guy I ever met!" she gushed. "It's just so nice of you to worry about Travis and Brad."

I swallowed hard. "Huh? What are you talking about, Amy?"

"I know why you said all that," Amy replied. "You don't think Travis and Brad can afford to lose a hundred and twenty dollars. And you don't want to embarrass them. That's so *nice* of you!"

"But — but —" I sputtered.

"So that's why you're pretending to be afraid," she continued. "You don't want them to lose all that money. That's so *nice* of you! I can't believe it!"

I took another deep breath. "So you'll cancel the bet?" I asked hesitantly.

"Of course not!" she replied. "We're going ahead with it, Craig. They deserve to be taught a lesson."

"But I *can't* climb into a coffin with a real corpse!" I whined.

Amy laughed. "Of course you can. I know it's no big deal. Stop pretending. I've got to go. My dad is yelling for me to finish my math. Bye."

I heard a loud click. The line went dead.

I sat on the edge of my bed, staring at the phone in my hand.

"It's no use," I muttered out loud.

Amy won't believe me. She won't believe that I'm a total coward — no matter what I say.

I've got to do something to stop this, I told myself.

But what?

The phone rang in my hand. I jumped up and dropped it to the floor.

Even a ringing phone scares me! I thought. Why won't Amy believe me? What am I going to do?

I picked up the phone. "Hello? Amy?"

"No. It's me. Brad."

"Oh, hi," I said. "Are you having trouble with the third math problem too?"

Brad didn't answer my question. "It's tomorrow night, Craig," he said in a low, solemn voice.

My heart started to pound. I nearly dropped the phone again. "Excuse me?"

"Travis says to meet at the same place," Brad replied. "At the funeral parlor. Tomorrow night."

25

Amy and I walked through the clear, cool night. A pale sliver of a moon floated low over the rooftops against a gray-blue sky. The trees stood silent and still.

We met Travis and his friends outside Travis's house. Then we let Travis lead the way to his father's funeral parlor.

Frankie and Gus tossed a tennis ball back and forth as we walked. Gus kept missing it and having to chase it over the dark front lawns.

Travis, Brad, and David all wore solemn expressions.

They mean business tonight, I told myself.

"Do you guys really have a hundred and twenty dollars to lose?" Amy called to them.

"Sure," Brad replied. "There are five of us. So we don't have to chip in that much."

Travis spun around and started walking backwards. "Do *you* have the money?" he challenged Amy.

"We don't need any money," Amy replied sharply. "We're not going to lose." She clapped me on the back. "Craig and I only have one problem."

"What's that?" Travis demanded.

"How to spend all that money!" Amy exclaimed.

Travis scowled and spun back around. "We'll see," he muttered.

"Hey — no tricks tonight?" I asked. "No one popping out of a coffin in a silly Halloween costume?"

"No tricks tonight," Travis replied. "We don't need any tricks, Craig. There's a real corpse in there."

David bumped me off the sidewalk. "Are you terrified yet?" he asked, grinning. "Tell the truth — are you, Craig?"

Amy lowered her shoulder and bumped David. He is twice her size — but she knocked him off the curb and sent him sprawling into the street. "Craig isn't even going to answer that question," she sneered.

We stopped at the hedges behind the parking lot. The funeral parlor stood dark and silent, as it had the other night.

But tonight, no rain. And no wind. Everything still. Eerily still.

Still as death.

Following Travis, we made our way to the back window. Our shoes scraping over the asphalt parking lot was the only sound.

We stepped into the deep darkness behind the building. Travis raised both hands and slid the window up easily. He motioned for me to climb in first.

I hesitated. "Is there really a corpse in there?" I asked in a trembling voice.

Travis nodded. "Yes. A real corpse. How many times do I have to tell you? He was delivered this morning."

"Still fresh," Gus joked.

But no one laughed.

I remembered the last time we came here. I remembered the big plastic bag delivered by the two men in the van.

I shuddered. I tried to imagine what a dead body looked like. What it *felt* like.

Travis glanced behind us tensely. "Come on, hurry, C-C-C-Craig. Get in. Before someone sees us." He gave me a boost onto the window ledge. "Come on. It's show time."

I took one last glance back at my friends.

Am I really doing this? I asked myself.

Then I uttered a sigh, turned, and lowered myself into the building.

26

The sharp, sour smell of formaldehyde greeted me once again. I covered my nose and tried to breathe through my mouth.

I heard a scrambling behind me. The thud of shoes on the floor. The others climbed through the window.

Travis clicked on a ceiling light and dimmed it. I squinted around the gray room. The dim light cast long, eerie shadows over the floor, like dark pools. I had the sudden feeling that if I stepped into one, I'd sink and never be seen again.

I shook that thought away and took a few steps toward the row of coffins. The lids were all shut. The polished wood glowed under the pale ceiling light.

I felt a hand squeeze my shoulder. I turned to

find Travis grinning at me. "What's your problem?" I demanded.

A mocking smile spread over his freckled face. "A little tense, C-C-C-Craig?"

I didn't answer. I stared at the row of coffins.

"I decided to give you a break," Travis said, still squeezing my shoulder.

"Excuse me?" I replied. "A break?"

He nodded. "I know you're terrified. We don't want to scare you to death!"

Some of the others laughed.

Big joke.

"So you don't have to climb in with the old guy," Travis continued, guiding me to a coffin in the middle of the row. "You just have to shake his hand and then give him a nice, cheek-to-cheek hug."

I rolled my eyes. "Oh, wow. Thanks for the break."

Hug a corpse?

Travis grinned at me. "If you just want to pay us the money and forget about it . . . ?"

"No way!" Amy broke between us, shoving Travis's hand off my shoulder. "This is too easy! Too easy!"

Travis stepped up to side of the coffin. "Okay. Whatever you say."

He motioned for Brad to help him. The two of them grabbed the coffin lid and slid it up.

I gasped as the old man's body came into view. I'd never seen a dead person before.

He lay on his back, in a black suit, white shirt, and dark tie. His arms stretched stiffly at his sides, hands clenched into chalk-white fists.

He had wispy white hair, brushed straight back over a speckled forehead. His eyes were closed. His lips appeared to be lipsticked red. His skin was kind of orange, not real-looking at all.

Not a joke this time, I realized, staring down wide-eyed at him. He isn't going to sit up and grab my jacket.

He's really dead.

I leaned over the coffin. Could I shake his hand? Could I hug him?

"Go ahead," Amy urged. "No problem — right, Craig?"

"I — I guess," I stammered.

David laughed. He pointed at me. "Look at C-C-C-Craig. He's shaking! Look at him!"

Frankie and Gus laughed too.

Brad stood down at the end of the coffin, near the old guy's feet, chewing his bottom lip nervously. The corpse's black shoes glowed like new under the ceiling light.

"Shake his hand," Travis ordered. "Go ahead. If you can."

I swallowed hard. I couldn't take my eyes off the orange face, the speckled forehead, the bright, lipsticked lips.

"Give up?" Travis demanded. "Can't do it?"

"I — I'm doing it," I insisted.

I took a deep breath and held it. Then I started to lower my right hand into the coffin.

I shut my eyes.

Am I really doing this? Am I really going to touch a dead man?

Yes.

I opened my eyes — and wrapped my fingers around the white fist.

Yuck. The hand felt hard. Cold.

It didn't feel like a hand. It felt like stone.

"Shake," Travis ordered.

I shook the hand. Once. Twice.

"Ohhhh." I dropped it and jumped back.

The guys all laughed.

"Craig did it!" Amy declared. "You lose, Travis."

I shook my right hand hard, trying to shake away the touch of the corpse.

"He isn't finished. It's hug time," Travis said.

"You don't win unless you give the guy a hug," David chimed in.

My stomach did a major flip-flop.

"You have to hug him cheek to cheek," Travis insisted.

Oh, wow.

How gross.

I have to press my face against that cold orange skin?

"Craig has no problem with that," Amy declared. "Show them, Craig."

100

Thanks for all the support, Amy, I thought bitterly.

I wouldn't be in this mess if it wasn't for you.

They were all staring hard at me. Watching. Waiting.

I had no choice. I had to hug the corpse.

I turned to the coffin. I leaned over the side and started to lower my hands toward the old man.

A loud creaking sound made me stop.

I stood straight up.

And heard another *CREAK*.

I turned to my friends. Their faces were startled, wide-eyed. They heard it too.

"What is that?" I whispered.

Another *CREAK*.

I glanced down the row of coffins.

And saw a coffin lid move. And then another.

All down the row, the coffins were slowly opening.

27

I let out a cry and staggered back against the wall.

Gazing across the room, I saw hands pushing the lids up from inside coffins. Swollen red hands. Bruised purple hands. Pale hands white as flour.

"We — we've *disturbed the dead*!" I shrieked.

The lid stood straight up on the coffin next to us. I heard an ugly hoarse groan. A green-skinned corpse sat up, turning its decayed head. It tried to open its eyes — but they were sewn shut!

The room filled with throaty groans and sighs like air escaping from tires. Another coffin lid lurched open. A corpse with a yellowed, rotting face began to lower itself heavily from its coffin.

Another corpse lurched to a sitting position across from him. I gasped as I saw the white worms wriggling out from his nostrils.

102

"Noooo!" Travis opened his mouth in a howl of horror.

"This is . . . impossible!" David shrieked.

"We disturbed them! We disturbed them!" I wailed.

We all screamed as a closet door swung open. The door slammed hard against the wall.

And hideous corpses fell out, staggering like sleepwalkers. Eyes sewn shut, their skin splotchy, falling off their gray skulls. Arms outstretched, they moved so stiffly, groaning, groaning from deep in their caved-in chests as they staggered across the room.

Toward us.

Amy screamed.

Travis and Brad backed up beside me, their mouths open, eyes wide.

I heard another gasping groan. And turned to see a corpse drop to the floor. His head was covered in a floppy, wide-brimmed hat. He wore a huge trench coat, many sizes too big for him. With another groan, he pulled himself up and began staggering toward us.

As he lurched forward, the hat tilted back. We screamed as his face came into view.

Half a face. Only half a face. Gray skin stretched over bone. A dead mouse clinging to his empty eye socket.

"Nooooo!" We all howled in horror.

But our cries were drowned out by the deep,

103

ugly groans. The gasping breaths . . . the hissing sighs.

A tall, purple-skinned corpse led the others. Head bowed, eyes sewn shut, he pulled one leg forward, then the other.

Suddenly, he stopped.

I let out a cry as his left hand fell off. It hit the floor with a soft *plop* and bounced under one of the lab tables.

The corpse paused for only a second, then came lurching blindly toward us once again.

"Let's get *out* of here!" Gus screamed, his face twisted in panic.

Too late.

They had us cornered. They had us backed against the wall.

I glanced down at the old man, the only corpse that didn't rise up.

Shuffling their heavy shoes over the floor, the corpses moved closer. Closer.

"Craig — *do* something!" Amy shrieked.

"Huh?" I gasped. "Me?"

"Stop them!" Travis cried, shoving me forward. "Craig — you can do it! You're the only brave one here!"

"I am?" I choked out.

"Yes! You win the bet!" Travis cried in a trembling voice. He was so frightened, so pale, all his freckles had disappeared!

"You win! You win!" Travis declared. "Just stop them! Do something!"

"But what can I d-do?" I stammered in a tiny voice, my whole body trembling.

"Do *something*!" Amy wailed. "You have to save us!"

She gave me a hard shove.

I stumbled forward.

And a tall corpse dove forward and wrapped its rotting arms around my waist.

28

"Let go! Let go!" I shrieked.

I squirmed and struggled.

But the green-skinned corpse, eyes sewn tight, maggot-infested hair down over its rotting face, grasped me tighter.

I heard the others screaming.

I looked up and saw them running — flying — to the back window.

David reached the window first. He dove through it and vanished outside.

The corpse wrapped its clammy hands around my waist. "Unh unh unh." It grunted in my ear, its sour breath tingling my skin.

Gus and Frankie scrambled over each other, squeezing themselves out the window at the same time. Travis vanished too. Amy followed. Brad dove out headfirst.

"Come back," I gasped. "It — it won't let go! Come back!"

"Wait!" I heard Amy cry. "Hey — wait! We can't leave Craig in there!"

"We'll get help!" I heard Travis promise, his voice shrill with panic. "We'll call the police!"

With a hard tug, I pulled myself free of the corpse's grip.

I scrambled to the window and peered outside.

And watched them all running across the parking lot, running full speed, running away in total terror.

I waited for about half an hour. Then I walked to Brad's house.

He must have been watching for me out the window. He pulled open the front door before I rang the bell.

"That was awesome!" he exclaimed.

I slapped him a high five. "Yeah. Awesome. Thanks for helping me, Brad," I said.

We both started to laugh. We slapped each other another high five.

I followed Brad into his living room. "Your brother and his friends were excellent corpses!" I declared. "They scared everyone to death!" I laughed. "Even I almost believed them!"

"They looked so perfect," Brad agreed. "All that disgusting green and purple makeup on their faces. The way they staggered with their eyes shut."

His smile suddenly faded. "Hey — don't ever tell Travis I helped you with this," he said.

"No. No way," I promised.

"I just thought enough was enough," Brad explained. "It was getting too mean. Time to end it once and for all. Besides, I owed you one for helping me with Grant in school the other day."

"Yeah. I'm glad it's all over," I sighed. I dropped onto the couch. "Be sure to tell Grant thanks, okay? And tell him to thank his friends too."

Brad chuckled. "Grant *loves* to scare people," he said. "I didn't have to ask him twice."

"Maybe we can all relax now and just be friends," I said. "I mean —"

I didn't finish because Grant came striding into the room.

"Hey, Grant —" I started.

Grant frowned at me. "Sorry my friends and I couldn't make it tonight," he said.

29

"Huh?" Brad and I both gasped.

"But — but —" I sputtered.

"What do you mean?" Brad demanded shrilly.

Grant shook his head. "My friends and I — we showed up at the funeral parlor. But the doors were all locked. No way to get in. So we left."

"Huh? You left?" I cried.

Grant nodded. "Yeah. There didn't seem to be anyone in there. So we left and went out for pizza."

"But — but —" I sputtered again.

"You mean . . . ?" Brad suddenly looked very pale. "The corpses . . . ?"

"Hope I didn't mess up your plans," Grant said. "Can we try again tomorrow night?"

Brad uttered a low moan. "I . . . I feel *sick*!" he exclaimed. "I'm going to *puke*!"

He clapped both hands over his mouth. And flew out of the room.

Grant turned to me. "What's *his* problem?"

"The corpses . . . ," I murmured. "They walked! They walked!"

30

Then Grant and I burst out laughing.

We both dropped onto the couch, giggling.

"We got Brad too!" I exclaimed happily. "He deserved it. He thought he was helping me out tonight. But I had to pay him back too."

Grant laughed till he had tears in his eyes. "Hey, any time I can scare my little brother and his creep friends, just let me know."

"Well . . . you guys did a great job," I told him.

"It was fun," Grant replied. "Did you see Brad's face go pale just now? He really believed my friends and I didn't show up at the funeral parlor. He really believed the corpses came to life."

"Good thing Brad didn't notice this," I said. I pointed to a glob of green makeup caught behind Grant's ear. "You forgot to wash off a chunk."

"I left my rubber hand at the funeral parlor too," Grant grumbled. "I'll have to go back tomorrow and get it. That hand comes in handy! Ha-ha! That's a joke. Get it?"

We laughed some more. I felt like jumping up and down, whooping at the top of my lungs.

I left the house, still chuckling.

What a great night! I paid everyone back for torturing me — even Amy. My plan worked perfectly.

The dares were over.

No more challenges.

No more kids calling me C-C-C-Craig.

I turned the corner and headed for home. Heavy clouds covered the sky. Somewhere down the block, a dog howled.

But I wasn't scared.

I was Craig, the hero. Craig, the *superhero*!

I knew I'd never be scared again.

I only wished the moon would come out.

Why did it have to be so dark?

About R.L. Stine

R.L. Stine is the most popular author in America. He is the creator of the *Goosebumps, Give Yourself Goosebumps, Fear Street,* and *Ghosts of Fear Street* series, among other popular books. He has written nearly 200 scary novels for kids. Bob lives in New York City with his wife, Jane, teenage son, Matt, and dog, Nadine.

Welcome to the new millennium of fear

Check out this
chilling preview of
what's next from
R.L. STINE

Headless
Halloween

Brandon, I saw the whole thing," Mr. Benson boomed. "I saw your little joke from beginning to end."

"Oh," I replied. What else could I say?

"Have you ever heard of the Golden Rule?" he asked, his caterpillar eyebrows going wild. "'Do unto others as you would have them do unto you.'"

"I never heard of that one," I muttered.

A group of kids had gathered around us in the hall. I started to feel embarrassed. Mountain still had his huge paw on my shoulder.

Some girls were asking Vinnie how he got all wet.

Mr. Benson leaned over me. I could smell coffee on his breath. Yuck.

"Would you like Vinnie to splash water all over *you*?" he asked.

"I tripped!" I lied. "It was an accident."

Mr. Benson's eyebrows jumped up and down on his broad forehead. He shook his head. "Brandon, I told you, I saw the whole thing," he repeated.

"He told me it was *acid*!" Vinnie chimed in. The little wimp.

A few kids gasped.

"Come with me," Mr. Benson ordered. He began to guide me down the hall.

"But I'll be late for class!" I protested.

"Too bad," Mr. Benson replied. "You and I need to talk. I'm going to give you Lecture Number three-forty-five."

"What lecture is that?" I grumbled.

"It's all about cruelty to others."

He led me into his science classroom and shut the door. Then he made me sit across from his desk.

He sat on the edge of his desk, hovering over me like a buzzard about to eat its prey.

"For the rest of this week, I'd like you to stay after school and clean the science lab," he said.

"But I didn't mess it up!" I protested.

He ignored that and began his lecture about this Golden Rule thing — about how we have to be nice to other people if we want them to be nice to us.

The lecture seemed to go on for hours. But I tuned out after the first minute or two. His voice droned on in the background.

I was already planning my revenge.

Mr. Benson, I thought, it's almost Halloween.

You shouldn't get on my case just before Halloween. Because now I have no choice.

Now I have to think up a nice Halloween surprise for *you*!

5

I stayed after school and cleaned the science lab. It put me in a really bad mood.

The last class had been doing some really smelly experiments. And now I smelled just like the experiments.

I kicked my backpack most of the way home. It was so late the sun was already starting to go down. Fat brown leaves swirled around my legs in a gusty fall wind.

Starting up my driveway, I had a really good idea.

I dumped my backpack on the front steps. Then I made my way to the side of the house. I climbed the wide oak tree that nearly touches the house. And I edged out on a limb right outside my sister's bedroom window.

I slid open the window. And I waited.

The lights were on in Maya's room. And her computer screen glowed. I knew she'd come upstairs soon. And when she entered her room, she wouldn't be expecting any visitors. Especially not from the window.

I leaned close to the house and listened. Yes! Footsteps in the hall.

I edged along the tree branch, closer to the window. Then I leaned back so Maya wouldn't see me when she walked into the room.

I held my breath and waited.

Maya stepped into the bedroom. I peeked in. What was she carrying? A bowl of something. And a glass of chocolate milk.

Perfect.

She took a few steps toward her desk.

I leaned forward . . . closer . . .

"AAAAAAAGH!" I opened my mouth in a terrifying shriek — and dove through the window.

Maya's eyes bulged. Her mouth dropped open, but no sound came out. Her hands shot up. And the bowl and glass went flying.

The bowl shattered on the floor. Potato chips flew everywhere. The glass landed on its side, spilling chocolate milk over the white shag rug.

"BRANDON!" Maya shrieked. "You jerk! You JERK!"

"Oops — just joking!" I exclaimed. I started to laugh. I thought I might keep on laughing for at least a year.

Maya started furiously pounding my chest with her fists. But of course, that only made me laugh harder.

"Okay, okay. I'll help you clean up," I told her. I knew I had to calm her down.

I was totally cheered up. It doesn't take much to put me in a good mood. Just a good scare.

"Promise you'll never do that again," Maya insisted.

"Promise," I replied.

"Do you *really* promise?" she demanded. "Really, really?"

"Sure," I said, patting her head. "I *really* promise."

It's easy to make promises. I mean, what *are* promises? Things that are easy to break — right?

I helped her clean up the broken china and the potato chips and chocolate milk. The rug had a big stain in it — but what could I do?

When we finished, Maya started getting her Halloween costume together. What did she plan to be? A princess, of course.

"Brandon, what are you going to be?" she asked, fiddling with the elastic band on a sparkly tiara.

"For trick-or-treat?" I replied. "I'm not wearing a costume. That's for babies. I'll just scare some kid and grab his bag of candy."

She narrowed her eyes at me. "You're kidding — right?"

I grinned in reply.

Why would I kid about a thing like that?

I lowered my voice. "Know what Cal and I are going to do?"

"Something horrible, I'd guess," Maya said, making a face.

"Yeah," I agreed. "Cal and I are going to trash Mr. Benson's house."

"You are not!" Maya declared. She picked up a pink crepe skirt and held it against her waist. "That's stupid."

"Why is it stupid?" I demanded.

"Because *you're* stupid!" she replied nastily.

"You're too stupid to be stupid!" I told her. If she wanted to fight, I was ready.

Maya dropped the skirt to the bed. "That house is too creepy," she said.

She was right about that. Mr. Benson lives in this big, old wreck, very dark and totally falling apart. The house is on the edge of Raven's Ravine.

"You know Mom and Dad said you're not allowed to go near the ravine," Maya sneered.

I repeated those words, mimicking her whiny voice.

She stuck her tongue out at me.

"Bet I could jump the ravine," I bragged.

She gasped. "You're not going to try it — *are* you?"

I grinned. "Maybe."

Actually, I had no plans to try to jump Raven's Ravine.

It was a steep drop, right behind Mr. Benson's house. A rock cliff, like a deep crack in the earth — about ten feet across to the other side.

It's really dangerous. But lots of kids have jumped across the ravine on dares.

If you miss, you fall straight down onto the jagged rocks below.

"Don't look for trouble," Maya warned.

"Thanks, *Mom!*" I snapped. "Don't tell me what to do — okay?"

She frowned at me. "If you go to Mr. Benson's house, you'll get caught, Brandon."

"No way," I protested. "Cal and I — we're too fast and too cool."

If only I had listened to her . . .

al called me after dinner on Halloween
night. "We're going headless, right?"

"Right," I replied.

"So I don't need a costume, right?"

"Right. You can use one of my masks to put on
your shoulders."

"We're not going to trick-or-treat. We're just
going to scare kids, right?"

"Right," I repeated. "And we're going to trash
Mr. Benson's house."

"Cool," Cal said.

"So hurry over, okay? It's already dark out.
Time to get moving."

I grabbed two ugly rubber monster masks from
my collection and hurried downstairs.

A horrible surprise awaited me in the front hall.

A kid in a shiny black Darth Vader costume stepped through the doorway. At first, I thought it was just a trick-or-treater.

But then, through his heavy plastic mask, he said, "Hey, Brandon." And I knew it was Vinnie.

"What are *you* doing here?" I demanded.

Mom walked into the front hall. "Doesn't Vinnie look scary?" she asked. She patted him on top of his plastic head.

"What is he doing here?" I repeated.

"You're taking him trick-or-treating," Mom replied.

I let out a groan.

"And you're taking Maya and her three friends too," Mom announced.

"Excuse me?" I cried. "I'm *what*?"

"You're being a good big brother," Mom replied.

"No way!" I protested. "No way!"

Maya and her three friends came bouncing into the hall. One of them was Ariel the Mermaid. Maya and the other two were all princesses. Yuck.

Maya was pulling on her cardboard tiara. The other two princesses were pushing down their crepe skirts and adjusting their glittery masks. The mermaid was tugging at her fin.

"Let's go," Maya said.

"NO WAY!" I screamed.

Mom narrowed her eyes at me. "I expect you to be a good sport about this, Brandon."

Before I could reply, Cal stuck his head in the front door. "What's up?" he asked.

"You and Brandon are doing a good deed," Mom answered. "You're taking these kids trick-or-treating."

Cal nearly swallowed his tongue. "We are?" he cried.

"Let's go!" Vinnie whined. "It's *hot* inside this mask. I'm sweating!"

Mom stood over me, arms crossed, staring me down. I could see that I had no choice. "No problem," I whispered to Cal. "We'll dump them as fast as we can."

"Okay, okay. Let's go, you guys," I declared. I led the way out the front door.

"Take good care of them," Mom called after me. "And don't let Vinnie get scared."

"Yeah. Sure," I muttered.

I led them across the front lawn toward the neighbors' house. It was a clear, cool night. Wispy clouds wriggled across the full moon like snakes.

The perfect night for scaring kids. But I was stuck with these babies.

The girls were giggling excitedly and talking nonstop. Vinnie held his heavy mask in place with both hands and trotted to keep up.

I could see small groups of trick-or-treaters all the way down the block. Cal and I guided Vinnie and the girls to three or four houses and watched from the driveway as they received their candy.

"This isn't any fun," Cal grumbled.

"Let's ditch the geeks," I whispered.

His eyes grew wide. "Huh? Just leave them?"

"Sure. Why not?" I replied.

"But they're only seven!" Cal protested.

"They'll be fine," I told him. "What could happen? They won't even notice we're gone."

Maya and her friends stood in front of an empty lot, talking to another group of girls. I didn't see Vinnie.

"Come on — *run!*" I ordered Cal.

The two of us took off across the street. The girls didn't even see us. We turned the corner and kept running.

After about half a block, I heard footsteps behind us. And Vinnie's whiny voice: "Hey, wait up! Wait up!"

He came running up to us, breathing hard under the mask. Breathing like the real Darth Vader.

"I couldn't see you!" he cried. "It's hard to see in this mask." He started scratching his shoulders, then struggled to scratch his back. "This costume is so itchy. And it's *boiling* in here!"

"Maybe you should have been Princess Leia," I joked.

Vinnie turned his black plastic head from side to side. "Where are the girls?" he asked.

"Uh . . . they decided to go on ahead," I told him.

Cal nodded in agreement. "Maybe you want to catch up to them," he suggested to Vinnie.

"No. I'll stick with you guys," Vinnie replied. "It's kind of scary out here. It's so dark."

Cal and I both sighed. We started walking again. Crossed a street. Then another. Vinnie kept running up to the houses, ringing the doorbells, holding up his Darth Vader trick-or-treat bag for candy.

"He's going to ruin everything," Cal grumbled. "We haven't been able to scare one kid."

"We'll dump him too," I replied. "I have a plan."

"But he's such a wimp," Cal said, shaking his head. "When he sees we're gone, he'll probably start to cry."

"No problem. Someone will feel sorry for him and take him home," I replied.

"But what will your mom say?" Cal asked.

I shrugged. "I'll tell her Vinnie ran off. I'll tell her we spent the whole night searching for him."

"Cool," Cal replied.

We led Vinnie to the haunted house at the dead end. It was old and creepy and surrounded by thick woods.

"We're not going to lock him in, are we?" Cal whispered.

"No. We'll just ditch him here," I whispered back. I turned to the mighty Darth Vader. "Go try this place," I said. I gave him a push into the weed-choked driveway.

The broken-down old house had no lights. I could barely see Vinnie step onto the front porch.

Cal and I took off, running as fast as we could.

We had only gone a few steps when we heard a frightening scream.

Vinnie!

Cal and I stopped. And listened.

We both gasped as we heard another shrill scream. Cut off in the middle.

And then . . . silence.

I laughed. "I guess poor old Vinnie met the ghost!" I exclaimed.

Cal glanced behind us toward the old house. "Shouldn't we go back and see if he's okay?"

"No way!" I cried. "He's fine. He just likes to scream. Besides, if something bad happened, it's too late anyway."

"But your mom —" Cal started.

"Forget about it," I replied. "Now that we ditched the losers, it's finally time for some fun."

I pulled the two rubber masks from my coat pocket and handed one to Cal. We both tugged our coats up over our heads and zipped them all the way. Then we propped the ugly masks on our shoulders.

"Headless Halloween!" I cried. "Come on. Let's find some victims!"

The Night Is Young...

GIVE YOURSELF

There's only one way out!

Goosebumps®

R.L. STINE

Everyone says the old Payne house is haunted. But you want to find out for yourself. Once you sneak inside, you'd better turn around and leave—or you'll never see the light of day again!

**Give Yourself Goosebumps
Special Edition #4**

One Night in Payne House

Get spooked at a bookstore near you!

Visit the Web site at http://www.scholastic.com/goosebumps